Argetlahm

A Swordpunk Story

by

Michael Joy

Part 1

Chapter 1

"Gol, wake up!" His mother called from the kitchen. "You'll be late for your final exam!"

Gol sprang up out of bed. "Oh no! Move Kewpie!" He pushed off his pet mole-bat which was sleeping inconveniently on top of him. He quickly got dressed, throwing on a tunic and pants as fast as he could and ran out to the kitchen to try to get breakfast before leaving for school. Kat and Kyra were still at the table finishing up their breakfast, their parents were already outside working the farm. He started stuffing his face and almost choked as he washed down his eggs with juice.

His mother patted him on the back to loosen the food. "Slow down honey, you're not that late. You stayed up all night studying. You have a great work ethic, but it won't do you any good if you're so tired you sleep through the exam. Here, have some coffee."

Gol took the cup. "Are you sure? Aren't I a little young for it?"

"Today is a big day, the exam will determine the rest of your life." His mother said. "I would say that makes you adult enough."

Gol sniffed the coffee and took a drink. "Bleh! That's awful! It doesn't taste nearly as good as it smells. It had better work or why do you drink it every morning?" He handed the cup back to his mother.

His mother laughed as she took the cup to the sink to wash it. "Okay, off with you and good luck!"

Gol and the girls went to the stable to get their silverwings. They lived on Gol's family farm which revolved around raising these birds. They were named for their wings which curiously had silver feathers in contrast to the rest of their body that was typically golden yellow, though rarely may have a reddish color or even less frequently black. Ironically, despite the name, the wings were not large enough for the birds to actually fly. They were large enough to be ridden by a full-grown adult, fast enough to be good transportation on their own and strong enough to pull carts and be used for other hard labor, not to mention racing which was a popular and profitable sport. The perk of farming the birds was that there were enough for the kids to each raise one for themselves. The default plan was that they were going to take over the family farm if they didn't pass their exams.

Kat and Kyra were daughters of farmhands that helped Gol's father, and their parents hoped one of the girls would be Gol's wife and help take over the farm. Of course, that was assuming they didn't pass their exams, which of course everyone hoped they would. But before they could focus on the exam, first they needed to get to the Academy. The three of them rode their silverwings down the road to town. It was mostly uneventful, but rather long, though nothing they weren't used to. Hopefully this would be one of the last times they would have to make this trip and then they would be able to move to live in the city.

When they arrived at the Academy, they left the birds in the pen in the courtyard along with all of the other rural commuters. As they left the bird pen, they ran into their classmate Zeke on the way to the exam hall. He was dressed nicely in sharp contrast to the peasant garb the three farmers were wearing. "Good morning, Kyra, lovely as always."

"Morning Zeke." Kyra reluctantly replied. "Sorry, we don't have time to chat right now, we're running late."

Zeke was much calmer than the others. "What's to worry about? I'm going to ace the exam and when I become an Engineer, I'll be set and then we get married, and you can live in my mansion in the lap of luxury."

Kyra tried to hide her disgust at her smarmy suitor. "But what about Gol and Kat? Don't they need to succeed on their own? Or are you going to take them on at your estate as well?"

Zeke laughed. "I'm sure they'll be fine on the ranch. Everything will be fine."

"We'd like more than fine." Kyra replied. "So please excuse us while we prepare for the biggest day of our lives."

With that, she turned her back on Zeke, entered the exam hall, and took her seat.

Gol shook his head as he walked past Zeke. "Desperation is very unbecoming."

Zeke's expression turned quickly. "Quiet farm boy. We'll see how this plays out by the day's end."

They all took their seats along with the other students. The proctor entered the room. "Welcome all to the Technocratic exams. Today is the day to prove yourself for all that you have learned, or at least should have learned, in your years here at the academy. When a young cyborg is born, they are incomplete, they have only their one right arm. They can generate electricity from their stub of a left arm, but no way to channel it, not until their cybernetic left arm is provided and their body complete, can they reach their full potential as an upstanding member of our society. Of course, these cybernetics don't just come from nowhere, they must be fabricated by Engineers and Smiths from materials that have been mined or salvaged by Freemen. In order to maintain the quality of this sacred work, so important to our way of life, we must evaluate every generation for the best and brightest. Those with the mental acuity to handle delicate circuitry will be Engineers, who will use their brilliance to not only craft the most critical technology, but also take up other positions of leadership and govern with their wisdom. Those who prove to have more physical skill will become Smiths and work the metals necessary to make the larger components of the cybernetics as well as manage all of the other metal work needs in the city. Those who fail either way will be Freemen, known as such because you will not be assigned a vocation, but rather you shall seek it out among the many other trades that do not fall under the jurisdiction of the Technocracy. Know that there is no shame in being a Freeman, there are many occupations that this society requires that do not require the strict oversight of the Technocracy and you will still be valued as long as you aspire to one of them. Shame is not in failing the exam, many will, only a few will pass because only a few can possibly have the skills required for such important work, shame is only in giving up on yourselves regardless of the outcome of these exams. I say this to remind you not to pressure yourselves to the point of distraction, clear your minds and do your best. The exam will be in three parts, a written exam, followed by an assembly practical exam and finally a manufacturing practical exam. You will begin your written exam here. My assistants have been passing out the papers and you will have two hours to answer all the questions starting...now!"

Everybody picked up their pencils and began going over the test. The written exam covered all of the subjects the students had studied, focusing primarily on chemistry, metallurgy, physics, and electrical engineering. It was important to gauge one's level of understanding of the tasks that would be required of them before placing such responsibilities upon an individual.

At first, Zeke felt very confident and thought he was getting through the test at a pretty good pace. The math-based questions were very straight forward, as were many of the science-based questions, but then there were some that seemed rather unclear, and he struggled a bit. As the test went on, the questions got noticeably harder and his pace slowed, but his confidence remained unshaken.

Then Kyra got up and handed in her written exam, the first in the whole class. She returned to her seat still seeming calm and appeared to meditate to prepare herself for the next round of the exam. Zeke was now shaken but resolved that his future wife would not outdo him. She may have completed her exam first, but that didn't mean she would necessarily get the highest score. He was sure that with her speed she must have made some mistakes. He shook his head clear of the distracting thoughts and resumed his exam, redoubling his efforts.

Then Gol finished his exam and handed in his papers. It had been quite a while since Kyra had finished her test, but still, Zeke had several pages to go and somehow Gol had finished his exam well ahead of Zeke and he was returning to his seat seeming just as calm as Kyra was. Zeke was much more nervous and frustrated and dedicated even more effort to finishing his exam.

Finally, Zeke got to the last page, only one more question to go. But just as he started to read it, he noticed Kat hand in her exam. She was as calm as her friends, in fact she seemed rather chipper even though she was the last of the trio to finish by a long shot. Still, she smiled, more than content with how her exam went, she sat with her friends. Zeke's frustration peaked, somehow three peasants from a farm had managed to outperform him on the first stage of their final exam. He was the son of an Engineer, one of the finest in the Technocracy, he was sure he came by the talent and intelligence to complete this exam and surpass rancher riff raff.

Zeke stared at the final page and tried his best to decipher the last question through his rage blurred vision and scrawled out his answer and stormed to the front to slam it on the table with the rest. Despite his feelings of victory, he turned back to the class to see he was the very last to complete the exam.

"And not a minute to spare." The proctor added. "Thank you very much Zeke."

Zeke was filled with an anger that was singularly his own among a crowd of cheerful and hopeful students. Nobody even seemed to notice his fuming. Everybody got up and moved to the next room for the next stage of the exam. This part was in the circuitry lab, which was large and clean with a table for each student filled with all the raw materials and tools they needed for their task.

The proctor spoke form the center of the room this time. "The second part of the exam is circuitry and engineering. Your task will be to assemble a hand from gears and integrate the touch sensors to the fingers and palm and attaching a connective adapter. Everything you need to accomplish this task is on each table with a few spare parts in case you make a mistake. You will be evaluated based on quality and function. You have two hours, pick up your soldering irons and begin...now!"

Assembling the gears was fairly simple, the structure was quite intuitive. The hard part was assembling the finer sensory circuits. This was a delicate process and having to do it with only one hand made it harder. The function of the hand was simple mechanics, but the sensory circuits were what allowed the user to feel through the hand, which was not only important for full touch, but also to properly determine pressure to apply when holding, gripping, pushing or pulling. Attaching the circuits wrong could result in inappropriate pressure and unnecessary damage, or a numb, stiff, non-functioning limb.

As they finished their hands, the students presented their completed projects one by one to the proctor. Each one attached the hand directly to the stump of their left elbow where their electric organ was located. This organ normally produced just enough electricity to operate a cybernetic arm, although some were able to produce a little more and were able to perform electrokinesis, though this happened to be rather rare and was irrelevant to this exam, only the operation of the cybernetics mattered right now. Sure enough, many projects malfunctioned, some gripped too hard and broke the test object, others could not grip well enough and dropped it. Fortunately, the four managed to succeed with at least somewhat satisfactory results. Kat and Gol were a little shaky and just barely held on, but Kyra's worked so perfectly the proctor applauded her. Zeke's appeared to work just as well, yet he did not receive the same applause Kyra did.

After everyone completed and presented their circuitry projects, they moved on to the third and final stage at the forge. The proctor took his place at the center of the room once again. "Your third and final task is to forge a chassis for a cybernetic arm. You have been provided with a hammer, an anvil, some other fine crafting tools if you want to get showy and go for some extra credit and enough ore to finish the job. You have two hours, starting...now!"

The students went to their workstations and began work. They picked up scraps of metal, heated it in the fire and pounded it with hammers. Again, this was difficult work for one-armed people, but they made it work, some better than others. Zeke had the most trouble, he was cobbling together scraps and only vaguely made a shape resembling an arm. He was confident he had done well enough in other areas he didn't need to excel here, just pass.

Gol used only two pieces of metal, one about twice as wide as the other. He carefully worked them into an almost perfect cylinder. It took him most of the time to finish, but when he presented his work, it was so near perfect the seams that joined the two pieces were almost imperceptible except to the most trained of eyes. The judges were in awe of such expertise from an amateur. "Never has any student made such a perfect chassis while still in a qualifying exam!"

Kyra tried a similar technique to Gol, but less impressive results, the seams were still clearly visible, but second only to Gol. Even Kat had something that was still better than Zeke's, even though it was clearly a patchwork itself, but still more organized, like leaves or scales, it was a work of art, what it lacked in function it made up for in aesthetic.

The proctor came forward once again. "Thank you all for your efforts, another exemplary class, we are proud of each and every one of you. Now proceed to the dining hall and eat, we are sure you have worked up quite the appetite and we have a grand graduation banquet befitting your accomplishments this day. We will deliberate and announce the graduates in one hour. Again congratulations, feast and rejoice!" The proctor and judges left the room through the door in the back, and the students left the room through the front door.

When they reached the dining hall it was indeed set up for a great banquet with every variety of food available in the region set up in the most magnificent buffet any of them had ever seen. Gol, Kyra and Kat stood in awe for a moment soaking it all in along with the other country kids. Zeke took to the front of the line and gathered the finest selection of each item, making sure to get portions large enough to get a good taste yet small enough that he could fit it all on his platter. He sat down with his platter and poured himself a glass of wine which he would drink very slowly. He gestured to Kyra to join him, and she brought along Gol and Kat much to Zeke's chagrin.

Zeke went through his filet mignon with truffle garnish and lobster with caviar and a side of steamed seasonal vegetables with delicate precision, making a show of how used to fine dining he was compared to others around him. Gol ended up with barbecue ribs and battered bass with a side of potatoes, Kat had similar tastes but passed on the ribs, Kyra had forgone meat and instead got a large salad with a side of vegetable stew with noodles. While Kyra ate as delicately as Zeke, Gol and Kat showed their country roots by digging in with such fervor they spilled a little of every bite and left their mouths covered in sauce. Even though they were the last to sit down, Gol and Kat were the first to finish.

Zeke rolled his eyes in complete disdain and disgust at the sloppy behavior of Gol and Kat. He turned to Kyra. "How can you stand such slobs?"

"Not everyone is born with a silver spoon in their mouth." Kyra said only glancing at Zeke, but mostly looking at her friends. "I would much rather dine with them than with you."

Zeke sneered. "Perhaps you will feel differently after graduation is finished."

"Perhaps you will be the one who feels differently after graduation." Kyra replied.

Before Zeke could reply, the council entered the room to much fanfare. "Congratulations once again graduating class! You have indeed impressed us here at the academy. We hope you have enjoyed your celebratory dinner. And now, without further ado, we shall announce the assignment of castes!"

The four had a hard time paying attention until their turn when they were called.

"Gol! Smith!" This was hardly a surprise, he stepped up on the dais and received his cyberarm with a smile of pride.

“Kat! Freeman!” Some looked on Kat with pity but she took her moment with as much pride as Gol.

“Sorry to hear you didn’t pass the exam.” Zeke said almost mocking her.

Kat shook her head. “It’s okay, I didn’t try that hard. I want to be a Healer, I’ve already been making arrangements with the Temple. This was mostly a formality.”

“Kyra!” Everyone paused with bated breath. “Engineer!”

Zeke spit out his wine in disbelief. Gol and Kat cheered loudly for her. “Congratulations!” Kyra collected her cyberarm and rank with quiet dignity, visibly blushing.

Zeke waited for his turn with growing contempt, worsened even more by the cheer of his companions each of whom seemed to be completely satisfied with their accomplishments.

“Zeke!” The pause between name and caste felt like forever as the whole world slowed down for Zeke. “Freeman!”

“Impossible!” Zeke was astounded and disgusted as he went to claim his cyberarm. “How can I be a Freeman? I am the son of an Engineer! I come from a long line of Engineers! I am meant to be an Engineer!”

Zeke’s father Cidolfas stood up from among the council that had graded the exams. “Silence! You are an embarrassment to the Technocracy! Know your place and accept your assignment with dignity!”

Zeke was still upset, but as he looked around the room, he suddenly felt self-conscious as he was absolutely the only one who was arguing with their assignment. Sheepishly, he sat down. The others ate cake in celebration, their first act with two hands, and yet Zeke could not lift his fork for a single bite.

The band that welcomed the council turned to playing dance music as the graduates celebrated. Gol and the girls took to the dance floor, taking turns with each other, the girls even took a few turns with each other while Gol clapped out the beat. It was so liberating being able to use two hands for the first time, but Zeke just sat and sulked. He had become so pathetic Kyra offered to dance with him. She extended her shiny new cybernetic hand. "Come on grumpy, how about just one song?"

Zeke hesitated for a moment before he accepted and danced. This was a moment he had been looking forward to for a long time, but now that he was dancing with the most beautiful girl in school, something was missing. After the song he drifted away from the group and stepped out of the dining hall.

Cidolfas followed his son out. "Son, this is most unbecoming of you. Today is the day you are supposed to become an adult and yet you are acting like a child."

Zeke turned back to face his father. "Why didn't I make Engineer?"

"Why do you think you should have?" Cidolfas replied coldly.

"I was supposed to be an Engineer, like the rest of our family." Zeke said.

"In the Technocracy position is determined by skill, not blood." Cidolfas said. "That is why you take classes with the children of the lower castes, because a cyborg is nothing until they have their cyberarm, neither good nor bad, they have infinite potential. We choose the castes based on what they can contribute, the best suited to the task get the task, those who are not are set free to find other work. Certainly, you don't think you presented anything particularly exemplary. If you want the truth, the written exam was your weakest section."

Zeke was shocked. "How many did I get wrong?"

"Far more, I'm sure, than you realize." Cidolfas answered.

"Why do we even do that written exam?" Zeke said. "The circuitry exam should have proven me well enough."

"Ethics and morality." Cidolfas answered. "The written exam is meant not only to test your knowledge but also how well you will use the power we give you as an engineer. There is a reason that we have to be restrictive of our technology, it can be too easily abused. The purpose of the exam is not only to determine who is best suited to carry on our legacy, but also to sift out those who could threaten the balance. The questions you struggled with suggested that you were not ready to bear the burden of being an Engineer."

"And you just let the council reject me over that?" Zeke said. "Couldn't you have put me through anyway? You just sat back and allowed your son to lose his place among the ruling class?"

"That attitude is exactly why you failed!" Cidolfas cut off his son. "You are a spoiled brat and allowing you to corrupt the Technocracy with your selfishness would tarnish our legacy far worse than failing the exam and living as a Freeman. I was the one who determined your caste. And if I had any doubts about that choice, you have just made it clear how right I was. Now, you have made enough of a scene, I think it is best you go home now."

Zeke was shaken and crestfallen. "What will I do now?"

"Anything you want." Cidolfas replied. "Anything but lead the Technocracy." With that Cidolfas left his son and returned to the party.

Kyra had not worried too much about Zeke, but she was getting exhausted by their long day. "Gol, Kat, it's getting late, do you think we should be heading home?"

Cidolfas had just walked by as Kyra talked about going home. "Excuse me, I couldn't hep overhearing, you three are from a farm far out in the countryside, aren't you? It is getting dark, I'm sure it's too far to go now. Besides, tomorrow is your first day in the Technocracy, you'd barely be home before you had to turn around and come back. You should stay at the inn for tonight, you will be provided more permanent lodgings tomorrow. All provided for by the Technocracy for your new roles."

"What about me sir?" Kat asked. "I'm a Freeman, I wouldn't be provided for, would I?"

"Kat, was it?" Cidolfas verified her identity. "I received word of you from the Temple pending the exam. They are happy to cover one night at the inn so that you can make your way to the Temple in the morning. Have a good night, and once again congratulations."

The three went over to the inn and got their rooms for the night. It wasn't much but compared to their farmhouse it was a step up. Kat couldn't contain her excitement. "So this is the beginning of our new lives? Tomorrow I'll be going off to the Temple, Gol, you'll be going to the Forge, and Kyra you'll be headed to the Bureau! I still can't believe you made Engineer! Our little Kyra is going to be at the top of the Technocracy!"

"Yeah, just don't forget about us little guys." Gol added.

Kyra laughed. "What do you mean little guy, Mister Smith? You are almost as high ranking as I am. Besides, I saw how you handled that metal, we all know this was what you wanted and what you were meant for. And you will be the best Smith the Technocracy has ever seen."

Gol turned to the window with his right arm around Kat holding his new cybernetic hand up to the stars in the night sky. "Yes, it's a whole new world for us now."

Chapter 2

The next morning the three went their separate ways. It was bittersweet, they knew they were going to better things, but it was the first time they were going to be apart in their whole lives. The ranch was where they were all born and raised, they attended school together, and now the results of their final exam divided their paths. Gol was headed to the Forge.

The Forge was where the Smiths worked, a network of furnaces and anvils where all the metalwork was done. The primary purpose was providing parts for cybernetics, but that only required so much time, so they kept their skills sharp by handling other jobs and determining the distribution of metal to what projects needed them. Gol rode his silverwing right up to the edge of the Forge and left the bird in the pen the same as he did the day before, only now he felt bad that the bird was alone instead of with his flock. With one last look to his loyal steed, he entered the front office where he would meet with his new mentor.

"Hello?" Gol called out. "I'm Gol and I'm reporting for my first day."

A large man greeted him in response. "Gol the prodigy? Pleasure to meet you, my boy! I'm Angus, and I'll be your mentor to train you in the ways of the Smith, although after I saw your arm chassis, I doubt there's much to teach you! Let's get started, shall we? Right this way!" The large man took him deeper into the Forge.

As they walked, they saw more Smiths working on various projects. Some were working on small projects like silverware and goblets, others were working on larger projects like pipes and furniture. There was one large area where gold was being made into jewelry and coins. Miners were delivering ore and salvagers were delivering scrap metal and it was getting distributed where it was needed based on quality.

"As I'm sure you remember from school, we only make cybernetic parts during graduation season and as needed for repairs." Angus began to explain. "The rest of the time we handle other projects. After graduation season, our next big project is the fencing tournament. We need to make sure everybody has swords for the amateur round and cyberblades for the experts. I imagine you know all about the blades in fencing, am I correct?"

Gol nodded. "Cyberblades are reserved for those who prove themselves as amateur fencers. Only by proving oneself in an amateur tournament can one be licensed for the installation of cyberblades for professional fencing. Prior to licensed installation of cyberblades, fencers are limited to hand-held swords."

Angus nodded back. "Very good. So now that you're here to join us, your first task will be to help us make sure we have enough swords for everyone." Angus handed Gol a hammer and tongs and picked up a set himself and demonstrated how to take a piece of metal, heat it up in the furnace, and shape it into a sword. The process was time consuming, and they chatted as they went. "Are you a fan of fencing?"

"Isn't everyone?" Gol answered. "It's the most popular sport, even more than silverwing racing or jousting."

"Would you like to learn the Smith style of fencing?" Angus asked. "You seem talented enough to represent the Forge at the tournament."

Gol paused for a moment. "Smiths have their own style of fencing? Does that give us an unfair advantage?"

Angus laughed. "Yes and no. The best fencers do use some trained style, or they never make it past amateur rank, it's not just Smiths, although I would argue ours is the best. We make the blades so we develop a style knowing the ins and outs of the blade itself and we make our own blades so unlike other fencers we match our weapon to our skill as well as match our skill to the weapon, and since we meet in the middle, we can be the best. On the other end of the spectrum, the Engineers have the least efficient style, too showy, all flash, no substance. They tend to prefer to be spectators of the sport, so when one actually gets interested, they usually think they are just putting on a performance and study moves that look better than they really are, but that also means when one gets good, he may be the best. Now the Freemen, they are the folks that try the hardest, because after you fail the Technocratic exams, fencing is the next path to glory and greatness. Hunters are the ones you'd have to watch out for the most. We live in a peaceful world and channel all of our aggression into sports, but the Hunter's Guild are the only folks who engage in real combat hunting wild game. They have more experience going in and they are the most motivated because being licensed for cyberblades is actually practical for their job. Aside from Smiths and Hunters, most people don't stand a chance of getting through the amateur league on their first try unless they actually take the time to study under another pro. Even those that don't study an established style develop their own through trial and error. That means that unless you study the Smith style, somebody else more experienced will beat you, so if you do think you want to give it a go, let me know." Angus stopped talking and focused more on hammering the metal. He gave the sword a few heavy pounds, lifted it, looked at it, turned it both ways, and sighed. "Still not quite as flat as I'd like on this side, a little crooked." He set it down and resumed hammering the metal.

Gol watched the technique carefully and checked his work too. This was actually something taught in school, although the practice of doing it with two hands was a little different. Still, he knew pretty much what to look for. He had studied a lot of metalwork, mostly tools around the farm, as well as whatever was available at the academy. He had prepared himself for being a Smith learning as much as he could about technique, shaping, and what imperfections could be a problem. A small dent may seem merely superficial, but it could be the weakness that leads to the whole thing breaking.

Once they got a blade in satisfactory condition, they would dip the hot metal in water to cool it down. Once it ready, they would set it down with the others and turn back to the pile of metal and started another. Soon they found their rhythm and were pounding out plenty of blades.

Angus got bored and decided to quiz his trainee. "So, how much do you know about cyberblades?"

"There are three types: finger claws, hand claws, and long arm blades." Gol answered confidently remembering this question on the exam. "Long arm blades are the focus of fencing as they are most similar, but the hand claws tend to be favored for close combat, finger claws are a last resort for expert level finishing techniques and otherwise tend to be used for everyday tasks rather than in fencing because they require more fine skill than they are worth in the sport."

Angus smiled. "I guess you do know a thing or two about fencing. You'll do fine, I can't wait to get you to the arena." Angus got up and inspected the morning's work. "Not bad at all for your first day, I can hardly tell which ones are mine and which ones are yours. I know you're the top student in your class on the Smithing scale, but how did a farm boy learn so much?"

"I paid attention in school because I really wanted to be a Smith." Gol answered.

Angus smiled again. "This is why it is important to teach all students at the Academy without bias, we must encourage all to their fullest potential because we'll never know where the next greatest talent will come from. If we ignore the possibilities and focus too much on the legacies of the past, we can stagnate and decay." His voice seemed to trail off as he began to think about something else.

Gol got curious. "What is it? Is something wrong?"

"Huh?" Angus shook his head. "No, nothing, nothing at all. It's lunch time, have you worked up an appetite? I know I have!" With the sudden shift in attitude, Angus led Gol off to the cafeteria to eat lunch. They went through the line and got potatoes and meat along with a glass of lemonade each and sat down at a table.

Gol did not recognize the meat, not that it was bad, just unfamiliar. “Would it be impolite for me to ask what this meat is?”

Angus shook his head. “No, not at all. But I’m not sure I can give you an answer. Most of the meat comes from whatever the Hunters find. We need our protein while we work, and the best protein is wild game, so the Hunters bring us back whatever they find. Usually it’s venison or rabbit, sometimes poultry.” Angus took a bite. “Venison, and pretty good quality, nice and tender.”

Gol started eating and found it did taste good. He noticed the meat was a bit spicier than he expected. “That is an interesting flavor, what is it?”

“Ah, imported pepper.” Angus answered. “You probably don’t get too much of the foreign spice on the farm, huh? Our chefs do like getting exotic flavors to mix it up a little.”

Gol thought for a moment while he drank a little more to cut the heat. “Unexpected, but not all bad.”

After they ate, they returned to their workstation. As they got there, their swords from the morning were being picked up. The man collecting the blades passed along a message to Angus. “Swords are on hold we have an emergency order for pipes. There’s a leak in the sewers and we need replacements. Here’s the order, make them as soon as you can and deliver them to the location on the note as soon as possible.”

Angus sighed. “All right, we’ll get right on it.” He grabbed his tools and indicated Gol should do the same. Angus demonstrated the technique for making pipes and Gol followed his lead. When they finished the manufacturing step, Angus looked over Gol’s work. “Again, for a first try, this is really good work.”

“I put in extra practice at the training forge at the Academy.” Gol explained. “I learned to be my best with only one hand, so with two hands I’m twice as good.”

Angus nodded with approval. “Good, emergency situations like this are a bad time to be stuck with anything but the best. Let's go!" Angus grabbed his pipes and Gol followed his lead. They went outside the Forge and proceeded to the nearest manhole to enter the sewer. As they went deeper, the light faded. Angus had a torch and lit it up so they could see their way around. Tiny shadows moved along the walls and underfoot with squeaks and hisses. "Watch your step, there are a lot of rats and snakes down here. Usually, Hunters clear them out but in the dark they are small and hard to keep track of. Oh, here we are."

"You got the pipes?" A rather unfortunate sewer worker was trying desperately to cut the flow of water, but it was still spilling all over his feet. Angus handed over the pipes and the worker got started on fixing the lines. "Hold that light a little closer please, right over here, thank you."

Gol had a look around. "What happened here? What did this kind of damage?"

"Sewer gators." The worker replied.

"Gators?" Gol shrieked.

"Calm down, the Hunters already cleared them out, or I wouldn't still be here." Just then, the rats and snakes scattered as a large shadow approached with a rumbling growl. "I guess they might have missed one."

"Where are the Hunters now?" Gol asked. "Is there any chance they could get back before this thing eats us?"

"No, we can't wait for them." Angus answered. "But don't worry, I got this. Hold the torch kid." As Angus handed off the torch, he released his retracted cyberblades and attacked the gator. It lurched back and dodged the first strike, barely getting grazed, but he shifted and struck the beast with a back handed attack.

"Good job Angus!" Gol cheered on his mentor.

"Behind you!" Angus pointed behind Gol.

Gol turned to see a second gator lunging at him with a wide-open mouth. He panicked for a second, realizing there was no time to think about what to do and he was all but defenseless. He put out his cybernetic arm and did the only thing he could think of, he charged up an electric pulse and released it, stunning the gator.

"Wow, you have enough juice to take down a sewer gator with one charge?" Angus asked. He walked over and gave the beast a kick, it was out cold. "That settles it, you're training for the tournament. Not everybody has enough extra electricity for shock pulse, let alone one that can take down a full-grown gator. That kind of combat potential shouldn't be wasted."

The Hunters finally showed up. "We're here, we got it...oh, we're too late huh? Well, we'll just clean up the bodies."

Angus stopped them. "Oh no, this one's his first kill, it's his trophy, we got this one, I'll let you take the other. Come on Gol, you grab the rear, I'll take the front."

"What are we going to do with this?" Gol asked.

"Plenty." Angus replied. "This gator is about your size, it's hide will make good armor for fencing, the meat will make a good feast, at least one, maybe more, and the rest is going to be a trophy, a nice housewarming gift for your new place."

Gol got a little queasy. "I don't know if I need the trophy."

"Okay, but at least the armor and the meat." Angus wasn't going to give up on this. "Nothing is going to intimidate the other contestants like you showing up wearing the skin of your first opponent. Haha!"

They emerged from the sewer somewhere different from where they had originally entered. Angus pointed out the butcher and tanner's shop, and it seemed like it was not just a coincidence that they happened to come out here. They hauled the gator into the shop. "Whoa, Angus, that's quite a haul you got there."

"New guy's first day and first kill." Angus chimed in proudly.

The butcher smiled. "Ah, so you want the first-time trophy special? Okay, but it's late, we won't have any of it ready until tomorrow, maybe the day after. But we'll let you know as soon as it's all ready. We just need his measurements. Hey Wedge!"

"What Biggs?" The tanner replied as he came out from the back room. He took one look at the gator and put it together. "Oh, which one am I measuring?" Biggs and Angus looked back at Gol. Wedge approached Gol with measuring tape. When he was done with Gol he measured the gator. "Yeah, that's just about right. I can have it started by tomorrow, but if you really want good quality, it will take two days after that. I'd say in the afternoon four days out."

"You guys look hungry." Biggs said. "How about some sausages to go?"

"Thanks." Angus replied, taking the food and sharing it with Gol. "We'll see you in a few days."

As they walked out, Gol had a few questions for the walk home. "You have cyberblades? I should have noticed the sheath slots."

Angus lifted his arm. "Yeah, I told you I knew about fencing. I used to compete, but I'm getting older, maybe just one more tournament, just to say goodbye. But I need to retire from the sport, and I just want to train one last champ to take my place."

"And you think that could be me?" Gol asked.

"I really do." Angus answered. "Well, here we are, you're new home. Your silverwing was brought to the pen in the front yard and I was told your parents came by and dropped off some of your things while we were working. Now go ahead and have yourself a good night."

"Thanks, and good night to you too Angus." Gol said with a wave as he opened the front door to his new house. As he opened the door he was assaulted by the familiar form of a beaver-sized golden mole with bat-like wings that weren't quite big enough to actually fly. "Kewpie! Now this feels like home. Wait until you hear about the day I had!"

Chapter 3

Kat left the inn for her first day at the Temple of Hinu, the God of Thunder. It was believed that long ago Hinu had created the cyborgs by giving humans the power of electricity and technology. After entrusting the world to the Technocracy and the Temple, Hinu ascended back into the heavens and ever since the Order of the White Magi took care of those who the Technocracy overlooked. The Temple had become a less important part of society over time, but their services as Healers were valued enough that they continued to do their work as needed. It was Kat's honor to take on this duty.

Kat was greeted by her mentor, an older Healer in full regalia. "Welcome Kat, I am Ruby. I am so glad to have you join us at our Temple! Come with me, the first step will be to get your ceremonial robes so that everyone knows you are one of us." Ruby took Kat into the Temple to a dressing chamber and provided her with the red trimmed white robes of a Healer. Kat changed her clothes in private and returned to her mentor in her regalia. "The next step is to get your carbuncle."

Kat was taken to a room full of red gemstones small enough to fit in one's hand. "Take one Kat, feel out the one that chooses you."

Kat did as she was directed, picking one gem out of the pile and holding it between her hands. She knew the ritual for the next step, slowly channeling electricity into the stone until half of it shattered and the body of some sort of light blue green mammal seemed to hatch out with the other half of the gem remaining attached to the creature's head. It looked up at Kat and squealed.

"Good, now you have your familiar." Ruby said as she reached for a wooden staff by the wall and handed it to Kat. "And to complete your regalia, your staff. Congratulations, you are now an initiate of the Order of the White Magi! Your duties begin with the garden where we tend to herbs that we need for medicine, and then we'll check the infirmary for any patients you may be able to help." Ruby led Kat to the garden behind the temple and presented the herbs. "I believe you have already learned the basics of most of our medicine, so you recognize which herbs are used for most of our medicine."

Kat nodded and demonstrated her knowledge. "This section looks like the kind used for antidotes to treat poisons and venoms from vermin. That section looks like medicine to treat eye afflictions. The lemons and cherries are for the throat, garlic is for the ears, and the aloe and oats are for burns and other skin afflictions."

Ruby clapped. "Very good, but I'm sure you know that we need a special base for our medicine, something which works wonders on its own, but is rather challenging to obtain."

"Mandragora." Kat said.

"Yes, you are good. Of course, we can't just keep mandragora out in the garden considering how dangerous it can be, so we keep it in the greenhouse at the far end of the grounds. The great glass windows let in enough sun for the mandragora while also keeping the rest of us safe from them. Before you go in, you must put on these earmuffs." Ruby took two sets of ear muffs out of a bin in front of the greenhouse and handed a pair to Kat and put the other on herself, demonstrating how they should be worn. Kat followed suit and they entered the greenhouse.

The greenhouse was filled with several plants that all appeared to be small herbs, but Kat knew better, there was something larger and hiding underground. The earmuffs rendered them silent, Ruby had to demonstrate how to handle them entirely by example. Finding one that looked large and ripe, she reached down and plucked it from the ground. As the soil loosened around it and gave way to the root, a small vaguely humanoid creature appeared. This was the mandragora, they were plants that looked almost like people, but the problem wasn't what they looked like, it was their sound. The little monsters could scream loud enough to give anyone a splitting headache. They were bitter little fighters who did not like being pulled from the dirt and would kick and scream until the very end. Ruby gave the creature a good smack with her staff, and it went limp before being stuffed in a basket.

Kat started looking for one that seemed ripe for the picking. She pointed to the one she wanted, then looked back to Ruby for reassurance. Ruby nodded and Kat proceeded to pull the mandragora. However, she wasn't quite ready for how much fight this one had in it, and it jerked her hand so that she bumped another mandragora, unearthing it in the process. The second mandragora pulled itself up and started screaming and running around, triggering other mandragora to unearth themselves and attack Kat. She tried to fight them off with her staff, but she quickly became outnumbered. Ruby and their carbuncle familiars jumped in and subdued the mandragora, then collected them into the basket. Kat hung her head in shame as Ruby lead her out of the greenhouse with their harvest. As they removed their earmuffs, Kat apologized. "I'm sorry I messed up."

Ruby shook her head. "No need to worry, everybody struggles their first time, mandragora are hard, but you'll get better. Now let's take these to the apothecary to be made into medicine." They returned to the temple proper and entered the back door to a room filled with tables with bottles, mortars, and pestles. Ruby pulled one of the mandragoras out of the basket and started crushing it with a mortar and pestle. Green juice squeezed out of the mandragora, and she poured it out into a bottle, then set it in the distiller. Ruby prompted Kat to do the same. Kat did as she was directed. They continued to process all the mandragora to make the potions and then collected the finished bottles. They each picked up half the bottles to carry to their destination. "Now we'll take these to the infirmary to help treat the sick."

As they entered the infirmary, Kat almost dropped her bottles as she saw who just stumbled in. "Zeke! What are you doing here?"

"Of all people." Zeke groaned. "I'm fine it's nothing."

Zeke had a black eye and was covered in cuts and bruises. Kat looked him over as she wrapped his wounds. "This doesn't look like nothing."

Zeke brushed her off. "I just had some trouble paying a bar tab."

"How can the richest boy in town be unable to pay his tab?" Kat asked.

"My father cut me off." Zeke answered. "I thought I had enough money to pay, but I drank more than I thought. They decided to rough me up a bit before throwing me out to make sure I knew not to come back."

"Well, we'll get you fixed up in no time." Ruby said as she put her cybernetic hand over his wounds. She released a mild charge of electricity that helped accelerate the healing of the bruises and cuts. Zeke winced. Ruby gestured to Kat. "Here, why don't you give it a try? Remember, low current, gentle."

Kat put her hand over Zeke's eye and tried to work on the bruise. "Hmm, I'm not sure this is working. Maybe we should try some potions."

"Give it a little more time." Ruby advised her student. "Just because you're accelerating the healing process doesn't mean you make it instantaneous."

"Actually, maybe the potion would be a good idea." Zeke interjected. "This stings a little."

Kat groaned. "It's your own fault for cheating a tavern. Which one was it anyway?"

"The Dragon's Bane." Zeke answered.

Kat almost dropped the bottle she was carrying. "The Hunter's Guild? Why would you go there? You do realize that's where Hunters go when they aren't hunting and killing wild game? Some of them hunt dragons and behemoths, you're lucky to be alive!"

Zeke looked confused. "Are they really that dangerous?"

Kat sighed. "You don't really know anything do you? I'd better go along with you to get this straightened out and make sure you don't get yourself killed for real this time."

"Why do I have to go back?" Zeke asked.

"Because they are going to make you pay eventually, one way or another." Kat explained. "The Hunters do not just let debtors go, especially if they know you come from money."

Ruby and Kat got Zeke fixed up and then Kat took him back to the tavern. The barkeep was not happy to see him. "You came back? Did you get the gold to pay us back?"

Kat put her hand on Zeke to stop him and spoke herself instead. "I'm afraid not, he has no money, but perhaps he could work off the tab?"

The barkeep laughed. "This is the Hunter's Guild, we only have one kind of work, hunting."

"Okay, what bounties are there for him to pursue?" Kat asked.

Zeke suddenly realized what was happening. "Are you volunteering me to be a Hunter? I didn't ask to be a Hunter!"

"You did when you skipped out on your bill." The barkeep said.

"Do you know who I am?" Zeke said defiantly.

"You're our newest recruit." The barkeep replied.

"I am the son of Chancellor Cidolfas!" Zeke stated.

The bartender remained unimpressed. "And if that meant anything your father would have come down and paid your bill. It's time to grow up kid, the first lesson is as soon as you got both your arms, you're on your own and your parents mean nothing. Now as for your first assignment, you get the same assignment as everybody else, clean out the vermin from the basement. Lots of rats and spiders." He led Zeke to the cellar and handed him a sword. "Good luck."

Zeke took the sword. "How big are these rats and spiders?"

The barkeep laughed. "You'll see."

Zeke went into the basement with Kat in tow. "Why are still following me?"

"Just in case you need emergency healing." Kat answered. "I thought it would be good for me to be nearby and ready to help."

Zeke grunted. "It's rats and spiders how bad can it be?" Just then he walked through a very large spider web and encountered a spider that was nearly half his size and shrieked at a pitch so high it was almost inaudible. "What in the name of Hinu is that?"

"That's a spider." Kat answered while smacking it with her staff and allowing her carbuncle to finish it off. "They get bigger the farther you get from the wealthier estates. Hunters usually control the population, not popular work, but the contract is good, so they put together an exterminator squad to handle it and make some relatively easy money. Mostly new guys in training."

"How do you know that?" Zeke asked.

"I took time to research options before the exam." Kat answered. "I decided on Healer after I realized how much Hunters get hurt and figured it would be good to be back up. That's why I'm actually here, part of my new duties is making sure other amateurs don't get hurt."

Zeke wasn't sure whether to be insulted, grateful or both. They continued through the cellar, killing vermin as they went. Zeke noticed the spiders seemed to get bigger the deeper they went. "Why is this place so big? What do they store down here?"

Kat laughed. "It's a training ground. They purposely left this place open so the spiders and rats can breed and provide us with a challenge."

"So far it hasn't been that much of a challenge." Zeke said.

"This was all just practice for the queen." Kat explained.

"Queen?" Zeke asked. As if to answer his question, they came upon a chamber filled with a massive web and at the center was a spider as large as both him and Kat combined. It hissed as it approached, venom dripping from its fangs. "I'm supposed to kill that?"

"Yes." Kat replied. "And quickly please before it eats us."

Zeke struck at the spider, but it deflected the blow with its leg and attacked with another leg. Zeke dodged and tried to counterattack. He dodged and rolled and tried to strike again, this time from behind. The spider was surprisingly fast and turned to face Zeke. They went back and forth like this a few times. Zeke got frustrated and yelled at Kat. "Are you going to help?"

Kat shrugged. "I'm a Healer, I just restore you after the battle and during if possible. What do you want me to do? Hit the giant spider with my stick?"

"Yes!" Zeke replied. "Throw the furball at it! Anything would help at this point!"

Kat frowned. "Did you just call my carbuncle a furball? That's my sacred familiar! I don't just throw her at vermin! She defends me!"

Zeke was exasperated. "Is she going to wait until I'm dead to defend you?"

"No." Kat replied. "But she will wait until you apologize."

"Are you kidding me?" Zeke screamed. He saw both shake their heads defying him. "Fine! I'm sorry sacred carbuncle, please help me here!"

The carbuncle frowned at Zeke, then looked to Kat who nodded and with what sounded like a quick sigh, she lunged at the spider and clawed fiercely at it. The creature was small and seemed very mismatched against the spider but moved very quickly to avoid any and all counterattacks while scratching the spider up until after a few minutes the spider started to bleed exposing weak points for Zeke to strike at. While the spider was distracted Zeke cut at one of the spider's legs and managed to cut it clean off. The spider shrieked in pain and squirted some webbing at Zeke binding up his arms so he couldn't swing his sword anymore. The spider tried to turn on Zeke for retaliation, but carbuncle jumped in front to defend him while Kat tore the webbing free of his arms.

More spiders came in response to the queen's cry. Kat started to swing at the support swarm of spiders and guided her carbuncle to help her. "You've almost got the queen, finish her off and we can get out of here."

Zeke looked back at the giant spider and thrust the sword into the wound from the severed leg and pierced the innards. The spider shrieked louder and flailed, moving so abruptly that it tugged the sword out of Zeke's hands. The swarm of spiders continued to flow in from the cracks in the wall and attack the hunting trio while the spider climbed up her web with the sword still stuck in her. Zeke tried to pursue the spider up the web but got his foot stuck. The spider turned with venom dripping from her fangs, clearly readying to finish him off.

"The web is a trap that will stick in some parts but not others!" Kat told him too late. With a very quick gesture, she signaled her carbuncle to free him. "Watch where the spider moves and try to stay on the same strands."

Noticing that his one hand did not seem to be stuck at all, Zeke hoisted himself up and threw himself at the spider as it lunged at him, landing on its back. He reached over to the sword sticking in her side and pulled it into a turn, tearing the carapace and all the creature's internal organs. Her legs flailed one last time scratching Zeke, but then finally went still. Zeke collapsed on the sword, panting.

Kat called her carbuncle back over to fend off the smaller spiders while she approached Zeke and gave him a carefully measured rejuvenating jolt.

"Whoa, that actually felt good." Zeke said.

"That was just a little first aid." Kat said. "You'll need a little more work after we get out of here, but that quick burst should give you a second wind to haul this thing back up into the tavern."

"Wait, I have to drag this back with me?" Zeke asked.

"Of course, we need proof." Kat replied. "Don't worry, my carbuncle and I will help you." They each grabbed a side of the carcass and she nodded to the opposite end of the body. "Grab on there." With a sigh and a grunt, Zeke picked up his end of the carcass and dragged it out of the cellar.

The barkeep saw them come out of the cellar and just barely cracked a smile. "You made it back alive! Congratulations!"

"You sound surprised." Zeke replied as he dropped the carcass for inspection. "And a little insincere. Are you unhappy we survived?"

"Honestly, my money was on the spider." The barkeep handed a bag of gold over to a patron he had clearly made the bet with.

"You bet we'd die down there?" Zeke exclaimed.

"Not both of you." The barkeep clarified. "We expected your Healer would make it back to tell us how far you got before you died."

Zeke grunted in disgust. "Well, does this at least make us even on my tab?"

The barkeep grumbled as he looked over the carcass. "Yeah, I guess, but just barely."

"Good I'm done with this." Zeke threw down his sword and stomped out.

Kat followed after. "Zeke, wait."

"Ugh." Zeke stopped and turned to face her. "What do you want?"

"Do you have any plans for how to make a living now?" Kat asked.

"What do you mean?" Zeke asked.

"I mean, you just broke even on a bar tab and you walked out." Kat replied. "What are you going to do next? You have no money, how are you going to buy your next meal?"

"Um..." Zeke paused. "I'll figure something out."

"No you won't." Kat said. "You're a hunter now, go back and find your next gig."

"I don't know, I think that kind of work is beneath me." Zeke said.

"You flunked your exams." Kat called him out. "Nothing is beneath you now."

"You failed too." Zeke shot back.

"Not as bad as you." Kat replied. "And besides, I didn't want to pass, I know where my place is, I chose to be a Healer. You're a brat, which is why Kyra and I never wanted anything to do with you."

"Then why do you care what happens to me?" Zeke asked.

Kat shrugged. "I'm a Healer, it's part of my job. If I don't help you now, I have to help you later, and at the rate you're going, next time I'll be too late. So grow up, go back in there, check the bounty board and get a job."

Zeke wanted to argue, but realized he had nothing. He had spent his whole life expecting to follow in his father's footsteps as an Engineer. He had no backup plan he had no other job. He might as well accept he stumbled into being a hunter. He went back into the tavern.

"You again?" The barkeep said indifferently. The patrons laughed.

"I'm just looking for more work." Zeke said as he picked up his sword and checked the board.

Kat came up next to him. "Let's start with something simple. Hm, how about this lost pet contract?"

"I don't know that one might be too dangerous for a beginner." The barkeep warned.

"A lost pet?" Zeke scoffed. "How weak do you think I am?"

The barkeep furrowed his brow. "Never mind, you're right, go for it."

Kat checked the posting as they walked out. "We need to go see a woman named Zamas. Let's see, she seems to live in the merchant district. Very wealthy, we could make good money on this one."

"What's this 'we'?" Zeke asked. "Why won't you leave me alone?"

"I already told you." Kat replied, still reviewing the bounty and not even looking at Zeke. "Part of my job is protecting hunters. I'm not done until you get home alive."

"Then why didn't you just let me go before?" Zeke asked. "You could have been done with me."

"Aw, that's no fun." Kat replied.

"Are you actually enjoying watching me suffer?" Zeke asked.

"No." Kat replied. "Well, maybe. Just a little. But you still need me."

"Fine." Zeke begrudgingly conceded. "But can you at least be quiet?"

Kat nodded and smiled mischievously.

They showed up at the client's house and knocked on the door. An older woman opened the door. "May I help you?"

"I am Zeke from the Hunter's Guild." He heard Kat clear her throat. "And this is my Healer, Kat. Are you Zamas?"

The woman's eyes lit up. "You must be here to find my Carrot."

"A vegetable?" Zeke asked. "No, we're here about a lost pet."

"That's my pet's name, Carrot." Zamas clarified.

"Oh, that makes sense." Zeke said.

"Poor little thing ran away into the forest." Zamas said on the verge of tears. "He's never left the safety of the house before. I do hope he's okay, I don't know what I'd do if anything happened to him."

"Don't worry ma'am we'll get Carrot back for you." Zeke said. "Now what does the little fellow look like?"

Zamas thought for a moment how to describe her pet. "Well, he's got big teeth, he's green with yellow eyes and orange tips on his tentacles."

"Tentacles?" Zeke echoed.

"Yes, he's a malbur." Zamas continued. "Did I forget to include that in the posting?"

"Yes, you did." Kat replied. "Zeke, maybe we shouldn't take this one on."

"Why?" Zeke asked. "What's so bad about a malbur?"

"They are actually pretty dangerous." Kat explained. "Their breath alone is one of the most toxic substances known.

The Order of the White Magi has a whole subdivision just for treating the sickness they cause."

"That reminds me." Zamas reached into a drawer and pulled out a pair of masks made of ribbons. "Here, these are made from treated fabric that will filter the toxins. You should wear them while you're looking for Carrot."

"Thanks." Zeke said, ignoring Kat's warnings. "Now can you just point us in the direction you think Carrot went?"

Zamas nodded and led them to the back door. "The forest over there is where he must have gone, but I'm afraid I just can't chase him through those woods, there are so many wild beasts out there. Oh, I do hope he's okay."

"I'm sure he's fine ma'am." Kat replied.

"We'll get him back for you." Zeke reassured her. "Safe and sound."

As they walked off toward the forest, Kat was unsure of her companion. "What are you thinking taking on a malbur? There's probably a reason this job was still left on the board."

"Are you really worried?" Zeke asked. "Did you see that woman? If she can handle this one, how hard can it be? It must be the runt of the litter."

"We'll see." Kat replied, exchanging a knowing glance with her carbuncle.

The forest seemed to be surprisingly empty, and quiet, too quiet. They could hear the birds up above in the canopy and the small insects buzzing around, the occasional woodland mammal scurrying in the underbrush, but nothing significant. Zeke's confidence grew as he felt more comfortable in the quiet woods. "See? Nothing to worry about. This is a cakewalk."

"I wouldn't be so sure." Kat replied. "It's always calmest before the storm."

As if on cue, they heard a series of growls and came upon a clearing occupied by wild creatures. There was a canine, a feline, an insect just as large as the other two with oversized claws, and what appeared to be a mass of vines with a mouth full of sharp teeth, the last of which appearing to be defending itself from the others cornered against the rock wall of a mountain.

"Guess which one of those is the one we have to bring back?" Kat asked Zeke.

"Judging by the tentacles, I'm going to assume it's the biggest, ugliest and most disgusting of the four." Zeke replied. "Why in the name of Hinu did she ever want that thing in the first place, let alone want it back now?"

"I don't know." Kat replied with a shrug. "But if you want to collect your bounty, we need to figure out how to get that thing back to the mansion. But first, we'll have to save it from the wolf, the tiger, and the mantis. Any ideas?"

"If we count your carbuncle, it's three on three." Zeke said. "So which ones do you think you can take? I'll get the other one."

"That's not a great plan." Kat replied, rolling her eyes at him. "But it is probably the best we got. You get the mantis, I'll take the tiger, carbuncle will take the wolf."

"You think you have better odds with the tiger than me?" Zeke asked.

"I think you're the best match for the mantis." Kat replied. "Do not underestimate those claws, your sword is the only thing we've got to match it. Tigers are different, I'll have to use my skills to handle it, and that leaves the wolf to carbuncle."

Zeke nodded. "Get into position."

Zeke, Kat, and her carbuncle positioned themselves to attack their targets. Zeke went first slashing at the mantis, which noticed him out of its large eye in time to move and counterattack. Zeke parried its claws with his sword. At the same time the carbuncle lunged at the wolf, biting its neck and clawing its back. As these two fights happened on either side of Kat, she relied on the distraction to attack the tiger. This was actually a hard task, because tigers were known for emitting sonic waves that confuse predators and prey alike and was most likely the leader of this patchwork pack of predators. Her staff alone would not be enough, no weapon would, she had to give it an electroshock to neutralize the beast. She dropped the staff in front of the tiger to draw its attention, then reached in with her cybernetic hand and gave it a stunning shock. She looked up to see Zeke had cut the claws off the mantis and her carbuncle had successfully subdued the wolf.

"Now we just have to get Carrot home." Zeke said.

"Hold on." Kat interjected. "I think I got this one." She put her hand up and emitted a low, slow pulse electric charge. It was hardly noticeable, but the frequency was just right to keep the malbur calm. "Okay, good boy. Ready to go home?"

Just then a figure appeared out of nowhere. It appeared to be human, but feral looking with no cybernetics, and almost no clothes, looking hairy and ragged with discolored skin. It lunged at Kat with his stump of an arm charged up with an aggressive crackling blue spark ready to go. She raised her staff to protect herself and her carbuncle rushed to help, blocking the charge with its hard armored head. Zeke came in to finish off the attacker, slashing him with his sword. The attack was somewhat clumsy, but Zeke caught him off guard and ended up impaling him. Zeke looked at the fallen figure. "What in the name of Hinu is this?"

"A gremlin." Kat said. "When people blatantly disregard the laws of the Technocracy, they are exiled and become gremlins, reverting to wild savages. They don't have access to cybernetics, so they live with one arm and learn to survive without the conveniences that civilized cyborgs like us enjoy."

"My father had told me about that, but I'd never seen one." Zeke said.

"Well now you have." Kat replied. "They are cautionary tales to abide the taboos and appreciate what we have. Generally, most people do behave, gremlins have always been those who experiment with things better left alone and the rest of us feel safer when they've been sent away."

"What could be worth a fate like that?" Zeke shook his head. "Well, we better get back. Come on Carrot."

Kat resumed her attempt to corral Carrot. Despite its fierce appearance, the domesticated creature was actually quite cooperative. The walk back was pretty uneventful, with much of the wildlife being even more afraid of Carrot than of the humans guiding it. The worst problem was every now and then Carrot tried to eat Kat's carbuncle and she had to stop him by gently tapping him with her staff, but otherwise it proved effective to lure him along.

When they finally returned to the mansion, Zamas came out to greet them through the back door, noticing them through the window. "Oh Carrot! I'm so glad you made it home safe and sound. I imagine you were so scared out there alone." She reached into the mass of vines to pet the creature under its mouth, and it let out a guttural sound reminiscent of a purr. Zamas then turned to Zeke and Kat, handing them a bag of gold. "And here is your reward, thank you so very much! And can you do me a favor? Don't let anyone else know about Carrot. Not everyone understands why I'd keep a pet malbur and if they knew I let it escape they would think I was even more crazy. They just don't understand what a sweet baby he is." She noticed they gave him a strange look. "I already put some extra gold in the bag as a bonus for keeping my secret."

Zeke took the bag with a smile. "Pleasure doing business with you."

They went straight back to the tavern and checked in with the barkeep. "Impressive. Honestly, I was sure the malbur was going to kill you."

"You knew?" Zeke asked.

The barkeep shrugged. "I tried to warn you, but you wouldn't listen. But you have earned my respect. From this day forward, you are a Hunter. Welcome to the guild! And by the way, I never introduced myself properly, but my name's Mack and I'm not just the barkeep, I'm the guild master."

"Thanks, I guess." Zeke replied. "I'm sorry, I'm tired. And I just realized I have no place to sleep."

"No problem, kid." Mack said. "All hunters in the guild are entitled to a bed upstairs any time they need it. You took on a queen spider and a malbur in one day, you earned a bed for tonight go rest. Tomorrow will have more hunts ahead!"

"Good night then." Kat said. "I have to get back to the Temple. I'll see you around." As she left the tavern, her carbuncle had her back, giving a warning growl toward the patrons, letting them know not to follow her out. The protective little beast prowled around her the whole way back to the Temple. As she finally got back home, she saw her silverwing in the pen out front and gave her head a gentle stroke as she passed it.

As she approached the front door, she was greeted by Ruby. "Someone has had a long day. Where have you been?"

"Babysitting Zeke on his first day of hunting." Kat replied with clear exhaustion in her voice.

Ruby cringed knowingly. "Oh, I think you've gotten enough punishment for yourself for one day. I'll show you to your quarters." Ruby led Kat to her bedroom. "I'll leave you to get some rest, I'm sure you need it. Good night."

Kat fell on her bed falling asleep almost instantly from exhaustion with her carbuncle curled up next to her. Her last thought was "I wonder how Gol and Kyra did today?"

Chapter 4

Kyra had the most intimidating prospect of all her friends, entering the Bureau as an Engineer. This was where the brightest minds in the Technocracy go to handle the most delicate and advanced technology and direct the most complicated aspects of society. The Engineers had a lot of power, but the purpose of the Technocracy was to make sure the most fit individuals held the positions to make sure the job was done right. Everything the Engineers did affected everyone else, successful endeavors made life better, and failures could be catastrophic. They tried to give people as much freedom as possible which meant that what they did, from cybernetic circuitry to urban architecture, was about maintaining a happy comfortable life for all. This was the weight of responsibility that now fell upon Kyra, a country girl who just two days ago held no higher duty than tending to birds in a coop on a farm.

Kyra was surprised to see Cidolfas himself greet her at the door. "Welcome Kyra, I have been waiting for you."

Kyra was flustered and unsure of what to do. She made a clumsy bow. "Chancellor Cidolfas. To what do I owe the honor?"

"You can stop with the formalities for now." Cidolfas replied gesturing for her to come inside. "You are my apprentice, and we don't have time for you to be so tongue tied all the time."

"I'm your apprentice?" Kyra said shocked. "How me of all people?"

"You got the highest score on your exams of course." Cidolfas replied, guiding her through the corridors of the Bureau. "I believe you may have potential to be the next Chancellor."

Kyra was shocked. "You want me to be Chancellor? I don't know if I'm ready for that."

"You aren't." Cidolfas agreed as he directed her into his office, closing the door behind them. "At least not yet. I'm not quite ready to give up my place yet, but I need to prepare my replacement long before I go. I had once thought it would be my son, but now that is no longer possible, I need someone else. Your scores on the exams were the highest in your class, particularly the written portion. Based on my review of your exam, you have the most potential of anyone since, well me. I know this may seem a lot but understand the gravity of being an Engineer. We hold the most powerful technology, technology that can easily be abused. Electronics have a lot of potential, more than many people realize. We restrict that use to cybernetic arms so that we may live full lives, but we must make sure that it is not used for anything else. The truth is that there are many possible forms of electronic technology, some indisputably dangerous, others seem more benign, but the biggest problem is how to power them. For cybernetics we use bioelectricity, which we have a plentiful supply of for that purpose. However, using other electronics requires more power than it would be healthy for most people to produce. There are other possible sources of electric power, but they are all potentially equally draining, especially if used in large quantities. That is why we choose to eschew it altogether, there simply is no other way to control it. Long ago, Engineers tried to figure out the most efficient ways to use technology, and after factoring the costs to quality of life, it was determined the best way was to simply forbid it. Some think this is unfair, and those criminals must be dealt with, but looking at the world and how beautiful it is as it is, it is worth protecting the simplicity of it all. Come look out this window and tell me what you see."

Kyra went to look out the window. The office was high up enough to look out on most of the city, yet not so high that she couldn't still see the people. What she saw was all the people going about their business. "I see merchants and craftsmen selling their wares, various customers shopping, Smiths and even the occasional Engineer organizing construction and maintenance. I see silverwing drivers pulling carts of goods and passengers and children playing in the streets. I see a normal ordinary day."

Cidolfas nodded. "Yes, a normal ordinary day. Everyone seems to be happy enough. Can you imagine any way to improve anyone's situation?"

Kyra looked around carefully. Everyone seemed happy enough, she couldn't see any problem that somebody wasn't already fixing. "No."

Cidolfas nodded again. "What if I told you there were ways to improve things that you just weren't thinking about? Any one thing you see out there could be improved with electronic technology. All the labor that those workers are undertaking could be easier with a machine, even the children could have fancy toys to play with."

"Why aren't we providing them with those things?" Kyra asked.

"That is a good question." Cidolfas replied. "The answer is as I said, any one thing could be improved upon, but could we improve all the things? Would there be enough toys to go around for all the children to play with? Could we fit all the machines out there to aid in all that labor? Would we be able to provide enough power for all those machines? Would they be able to afford all of that? After all, we can't just create those machines for free. The balance of our society, the Engineers and Smiths working together to create cybernetics, even Freemen providing the most basic resources so we can do our work, all of it requires some work from everyone involved. Creating more technology means pulling more people from those tasks and resources as well. Every circuit, every wire, every gear, every metal plate used in a chassis, all of that must be taken away from what we already use. We could improve any one thing out there, but to try to improve all of them would lead to an imbalance in which other things would have to be sacrificed. We have determined that we have reached a certain equilibrium, and to go beyond would be nothing more than the blind hubris of the Engineers to prove what we are capable of with no regard to the price those happy people would have to pay to see what we can do. Machines could make labor easier, but it could put craftsmen out of work. Children could get better toys, but they would be less motivated to enjoy the freedom of youth. Even in the best-case scenario, the raw materials would be a drain in the long run. People would want more, but when would they get enough? When one understands the mechanics of what we can create, we can dream of infinite possibilities, but the reality is our world has finite resources and we simply cannot chase all those dreams. Therefore, it is the responsibility of Engineers, and the Chancellor in particular, to abide by the Great Taboo of technology, restrict electronics to cybernetics, and channel the intelligence and creativity of our greatest minds into more practical endeavors. The Chancellor must be one who recognizes the greater good and puts the peace of the people above blind ambition."

Cidolfas walked away from the window to pick up some documents from his desk and beckoned Kyra to follow. "We must now go to the Court of Trials where we will review the cases of Engineers who have developed new technologies. You are familiar with the work Engineers usually do, but there is unfortunately a harsher side as well." They proceeded to leave the office and walk down another corridor to the court room.

The court was a large hall filled with enough seating for a large audience. They had entered from the head of the room where Cidolfas would sit with his panel of judges to consider the cases of new inventors who had produced questionable technology. Cidolfas greeted the other judges. "Sorry I'm late, I had to welcome the new girl." They all chuckled knowingly. Cidolfas directed Kyra to take a seat off to the side. "Watch, listen, learn, but say nothing." Kyra nodded as Cidolfas took his seat at the center of the panel. "Bring in the first case."

A man entered the room wheeling in a cart carrying what appeared to be a machine, but Kyra had no idea what type of machine this was. The panel did not know either because they asked. "Wain, what is the invention you have brought before us?"

"It is a combustion engine." The man called Wain replied as documents were passed out to the panel. "It is a key component to be used in motorized vehicles. The idea is that they will be like carriages but without the need to be pulled by animals, and they will be able to go faster and pull heavier loads."

"Very interesting prospect." Cidolfas commented. "What fuels it?"

The man twitched nervously and began to sweat. "Petroleum oil."

A collective gasp was just barely audible from the panel. "Petroleum oil is very difficult to obtain. We have occasionally found it in mines, but the liquid cannot be safely collected without potentially contaminating the surrounding environment. Farms and water sources could be damaged affecting food supplies. Furthermore, this engine that would be powered by that substance would convert it into toxic gas, if I am reading this report correctly."

Wain lowered his head. "I'm afraid that would be true sir. But the efficiency of motion would be well worth it."

"Efficiency of motion at the expense of land, water, and air." Cidolfas pointed out. "The more this device would be used, the more damage would be done to living creatures in our food chain including ourselves directly. Isn't it true that if these combustion engines were allowed to operate within any civilized area, the exhaust would compromise the quality of breathable air?"

"Well..." Wain began to stammer, looking around at all the panelists, looking for mercy and finding none. "Yes."

Cidolfas looked to each side exchanging looks with his colleagues. "We cannot allow this. While we concede the technology has its benefits, they are currently outweighed by the damage that can be done by it. Therefore, we are currently banning the use of this engine. However, you will be allowed to continue to do research into an alternative method of powering your motor vehicles that does not have the same drawbacks as your current technology."

The crestfallen man wheeled his cart out.

"Next case please." Cidolfas called out.

The next man came in with a similar cart except that instead of a machine it was a model of a miniature building on top of a metal box.

"Duke, was it?" Cidolfas asked. "And what is your project?"

"A power generator." The man called Duke replied. "It will produce enough electricity to operate machines throughout the city, and possibly into the surrounding countryside."

"And what fuels it?" Cidolfas asked.

Duke was caught off guard by the question, suddenly going silent and tapping the box as he searched for an answer. "Um...that would be...small...very small...and very, very controlled, um...fission explosions..." There was an audible collective gasp from the council which Duke tried to ignore as he powered through to finish his thought. "...of...an isotope of...uranium." More gasping on "isotope" and "uranium" the latter getting the louder gasp, followed by muttering.

Cidolfas banged his gavel to get everyone quiet and focused. "Uranium? You mean you want to purposely detonate one of the most dangerous materials we know of? The material that has been found to radiate energy that is known to cause damage to anything living or not that isn't protected by lead. Wait, is that box lead? Did you actually bring uranium into the court?"

Duke was caught off guard and paused. "Maybe...perhaps...yes."

"Are you mad?" Cidolfas asked. "And according to your notes everyone else working on the project died from radiation sickness. I think it should go without saying this project is banned! We will deliberate on your fate later but for now, get that out of here and find a proper way to dispose of it!"

Duke was promptly escorted out of the courtroom along with his invention.

The panel of judges were quite flustered, upset by the prospect of being exposed to radiation from the uranium. They took a moment to gather themselves before Cidolfas called for the next case. "Bring in the next inventor please."

Four people entered the courtroom. One was holding what appeared to be a long, hollow, metal rod, another was in chains being flanked by the other two who were clearly guards.

"Please explain your invention, Colt." Cidolfas requested.

"I call it a gun." The man in chains named Colt replied. "Inside the metal barrel, a small projectile I call a bullet is packed against a volatile powder. On the other side of that powder is a trigger to ignite the powder and create a small but sufficient explosion to propel the bullet."

"To what end?" Cidolfas asked.

"To kill." Colt answered to a loud and noisy reaction from the council. Clearly everyone was upset, but he raised his hand to try to calm them as if they were overreacting to his initial statement. "This is a weapon for Hunters."

"Explain how this is any more efficient than a bow and arrow or electrokinesis." Cidolfas asked. "Both methods seem to serve our Hunters well for pursuing their quarry at range. To approve this, I need to know why it is better."

Colt glanced at the gun and then back at the judges. "Speed, it can be loaded beforehand, ready to fire immediately upon finding quarry instead of fumbling to notch an arrow to a bow. Accuracy, the barrel focuses the bullet even more efficiently than a bow can be aimed. Power, the force is concentrated on the projectile which is smaller than an arrow and more focused than an electrokinetic bolt. More force in one spot upon impact will allow Hunters a distinct advantage against the most powerful beasts. Even the natural armor of dragon scales will be no match for a gun." The man's hands were shaking with anticipation.

Cidolfas remained unimpressed. "It sounds dangerous, and unnecessarily so. The Hunters have enough weapons in their arsenal, there is no need for this. The explosive component suggests an extra danger and unnecessary risk to the handler and the speed at which it can be readied for use only increases the risk that it will be misused against civilians."

"I don't think you fully appreciate what this device is capable of." Colt interjected. "Perhaps a demonstration is in order." In a surprise move he dropped into a split and kicked the guards' feet out from under them, then whipping them both with his chains in one fluid motion. He carried the momentum into striking the third guard holding the gun, causing the guard to fumble and throw it in the air. The chained inventor caught his gun in the air and pointed it at Cidolfas and pulled the trigger, only to find nothing happened.

Cidolfas remained surprisingly calm through all of this. "You didn't think we would be so careless as to actually allow the gun to be loaded in the court, did you?"

The angry gunslinger adjusted his grip putting his cybernetic hand forward on the metal shaft and released a precision electric bolt directly at the chancellor. Cidolfas raised his own cybernetic hand and countered the bolt with a charge of his own.

"Blind rage, predictable." Cidolfas commented. "We already had doubts about this weapon to begin with, hence the extra security measures taken. I hoped you would have at least had the logic to understand that acting out like this would hurt your case and at least pretend to take it calmly and demonstrate reason to try to convince us the gun is not as dangerous as we suspected. But this attempted assassination proves beyond the shadow of a doubt that this is too dangerous to allow. Not only is the project banned, but you are sentenced to exile, with immediate disarmament."

The guards took the gun from Colt, and then took a hold of his cybernetic arm and tore it off, applying liquid rubber to his stump to prevent use of electricity. The man screamed and whimpered but got no sympathy from anyone.

Cidolfas straightened himself out and took a seat. "I think it's appropriate we take a recess. Once we have had some time to clear our minds, let us reconvene on the matter of the nuclear reactor and how we handle that inventor. Personally, I'm leaning towards exile, but I sense good intentions despite poor execution, and would like for us to consider his matter more carefully before sentencing him. I think we can all agree we do not have that clarity at the moment." The others nodded in agreement. "Very well, I shall see you in three hours. Kyra, come along with me."

Cidolfas got up to leave and Kyra followed him out. She was stunned into silence by what she had witnessed and took some time to collect herself enough to speak to her mentor. "I didn't know that's what criminals were like. Such range of personalities and motivations."

Cidolfas nodded. "Yes, that's the difficulty of the judgement aspect of this caste. Evil is a simple concept in children's tales, but in reality, nobody simply chooses evil, it is the result of good intentions that are implemented in the wrong ways. Sometimes the frustration of attempting to improve things without understanding why it's not an improvement leads one to make mistakes that lead one down the wrong path. When one refuses to learn the error of their ways, that is when they must have reason forced upon them. That is when we must make the harsh judgement of exile. It is an extreme sentence that is not to be taken lightly. To exile someone is to cut them off from all conveniences of modern society, including a cybernetic arm. The exiles, gremlins as they are often called by the Hunters and others on the edge of society that may come across them, live as feral savages. Some do not survive at all. Therefore, that punishment is only reserved for those who cannot be trusted to live among civilized folks. A stern hand is required for this job, but also mercy as well, as otherwise one would be no better than those that one judges."

"I notice that all the cases regarded inventors presenting inventions." Kyra observed. "Do any of those inventions ever get approved?"

Cidolfas did not answer right away, the first hesitant pause to interrupt his otherwise confident air. "I want to show you something." Without another word, he led Kyra to the stables to get their silverwings to ride. Where they were riding to, Kyra couldn't even begin to guess.

They rode through the streets to the edge of the city and out into the open countryside. Kyra was not familiar with this territory. It was the other side of the city from the farm where she had lived her whole life up until this point. She was raised a farmhand and a student, she was not an adventurer and the wilderness on the other side of the city was uncharted territory to her, especially where they were headed right now. Cidolfas was leading them into a place that nobody ever went. That was painfully clear from the growth of foliage that blocked any visible path, and yet Cidolfas pressed on as if he knew exactly where he was going and what he was doing.

They travelled deep into the forest, the trees blocking out the view of the path behind them and the entire civilized world. Kyra was a little scared she had no idea where she was, and now she was alone with a man she knew very little of before today and the last words they exchanged had not put her in the best light.

Finally, after what seemed like forever, in the depths of the wild forest, they came upon a large, long building. Cidolfas dismounted his bird and gestured for Kyra to do so as well. He opened the door to the building. The inside was one huge room that appeared to hold a large boat.

"What is this?" Kyra asked.

"This is an airship." Cidolfas answered. "I know it appears to be a boat, but this vessel was not designed to float in water, it was made to float in the sky. The problem is that it takes a lot of power to make it work, and there is no known source of such power that can safely keep it aloft that would be worth using for such a purpose."

"This is banned technology." Kyra guessed.

"Yes." Cidolfas confirmed.

"What happened to the inventor?" Kyra asked. "Did you exile him?"

Cidolfas laughed a sad laugh. "No. He wasn't exiled. It was me. In my youth, I had been ambitious enough to think I could change the world with this technology. I myself was brought before the court. I was judged and held responsible for my actions. My workshop was closed and hidden away. I keep it only to remind myself of my failures and to keep perspective as I judge others. Learning from that, I started from a bad place but learned how to be a fair and just chancellor. To answer the question you asked earlier, no, the inventions do not ever get approved. It's not about the inventions themselves, it's never about the inventions, there is no room for new technology, if you are brought up to court the invention has already been determined taboo. The trial is about the inventor, to determine whether one may be redeemed as I was, or if they are beyond hope and must be exiled for the greater good. Wain, the one who wanted to make a combustion engine had the noble intent of improving transportation, as I did, perhaps that's why I went easy on him. Colt, the one who wanted to make a gun was violent, and he will invariably channel that violent energy into something bad. As for Duke, the one working on nuclear power, that one is truly unclear. On one hand he is reckless and dangerous and has sacrificed his cohorts for his research. However, on the other hand, if he were to succeed, that power supply would allow for technology like this to work, but then again, it could be used to power technology more rightfully forbidden. The question that we must consider before we face him again, is whether his intentions are to help make the world better, or just to allow the impossible to become possible for the sake of proving that he can. Is it about the greater good, or just his pride?"

Cidolfas led her back outside to remount their birds and ride back to the city. They arrived in enough time for a meal before the court gathered again. They went to a restaurant where Cidolfas ordered for both of them. They were served small portions of poultry in a mushroom sauce with a side of steamed vegetables and a glass of wine each. "We've seen a lot today, it would do good to ease our minds just a little." Cidolfas was very quietly enjoying a standard meal for him, but Kyra was in awe of everything, and he allowed her to take it in. She had never been to such a nice restaurant, it was definitely a high end establishment. There were silk table cloths on every table, silverware made from real silver, and drinks were served in crystal goblets. The staff appeared to be dressed better than anything Kyra had been familiar with. This was the sort of private business where the Freemen caste did well for themselves, it was assumed that the Engineers and Smiths lived better than the other caste, but there were many things even they needed that they could not provide for themselves that Freemen could get their cut of the wealth as long as they knew how to provide worthwhile service. A number of farms like the one Kyra came from supported this restaurant by selling them the food they needed to operate like this and through the added value of presentation and skilled chefs they elevated themselves to a higher tier. Kyra was ashamed to admit to herself she had been envious of these people when she was growing up, always wondering if she would be anything more than a simple farm girl. It took all she had in her to try to keep her composure while she ate her meal and tried not to embarrass herself or show her lack of experience in such a setting.

After they finished their meal they returned to the bureau. They both dreaded what was coming next as they returned to the court, although of course Cidolfas was not showing it. He had become quite used to his duties and passing judgement on criminals, but he was always aware that he was deciding people's lives, and the weight of that on his heart never got any lighter. The only consolation was that he had the chance to deliberate with his fellow judges and let them take some of the burden off of his mind.

They all gathered in the court with Duke in attendance to be questioned and offered a chance to defend himself. Duke had been asked to explain how he had come up with the reactor and he obliged. "Uranium is usually an unwanted by product of mining, occasionally found alongside more desirable metal ores. Many years ago, it was discovered that this metal radiates invisible but deadly energy that hurts those who are exposed to it, and it was forbidden for Smiths to work with it. Since then, we have been working with miners to isolate this toxic metal and dispose of it responsibly. Much research has had to go into figuring out how to properly dispose of it. The most effective methods include storing inside lead and vitrification into glass, and both at the same time is preferable. But as we have performed these disposal processes on this substance, we have also experimented with more efficient methods. One of these experiments led to the discovery that we could generate energy under certain circumstances, a chain reaction that occurred when vitrification went wrong. The energy output is significantly greater than standard bioelectric output and could operate several machines, including those that were banned only because we did not have suitable power sources. Of course, as standard procedure, I had to submit my research into what we stumbled upon before going forward with anything large scale."

One of the other judges commented. "The data you have brought before us suggests that this process is in itself very risky not only because of the toxic material which requires lead suits to even mitigate exposure, but also because this process involves purposely causing the materials to explode in small, controlled circumstances which by your own admission was discovered by accident and is extremely volatile to the point that calling them controlled at all is an overstatement. Based on what incidental data you have collected, do you believe you can refine this process in any way that is safe in the foreseeable future?"

Duke closed his eyes, hung his head and sighed. "To be honest, it does not seem likely that I will be able to correct this problem without significant loss beyond what the council finds acceptable. I do have a theory that there may be a way I can reduce some of the adverse effects, but I'm not sure yet if it can be practically implemented and the math is not clear if such restriction might also diminish the energy returns to the point that it may not be worthwhile at all."

Cidolfas nodded. "I appreciate your honesty. I notice that one of the methods of mitigating the adverse effects of the nuclear reactor is cooling the hot uranium with water which not only releases boiling water to the external systems, but also introduces trace amounts of radiation as well. This environmental impact cannot be ignored. In the spirit of honesty which you have demonstrated, can you tell me that you have any way to mitigate that?"

Duke shook his head. "I am sorry sir, I have no way of guaranteeing that I can resolve that either."

Cidolfas nodded and looked to his colleagues. "Does anyone have any further questions?" Everyone shook their heads. "Then I believe it is time to decide your fate. The project in itself will of course be banned under the Great Taboo. You, Duke, however, have demonstrated honesty and integrity, presenting your findings before doing irreparable damage. I am a little concerned that you brought a sample of uranium into the court, even if it was properly contained, and that your team is dead and wonder if you would have come forth if you knew you had anyone left to sacrifice in the name of science. I find this too difficult to make up my mind alone, so I will defer to the council. We will now write down our votes of mercy or exile, the majority shall decide your fate."

As Cidolfas said, his twelve colleagues wrote down their votes, folded the papers, and passed them to him to read anonymously. "There are twelve votes, if there is a tie, it falls to me to cast the deciding vote. Mercy. Exile. Mercy. Exile. Mercy. Exile. Mercy. Exile. Mercy. Exile. Mercy. That is eleven votes, six Mercy, five exile. If the next and final vote is exile, it will be a tie and it will fall on me to break the tie and decide your fate, if it is mercy, you will win a majority vote, however narrowly, and be free to go." Cidolfas unfolded the final ballot and everyone quivered with anxiety over this final result. "Mercy. Congratulations, Duke you are free to go. But please remember that you cannot experiment with uranium and when you are put on disposal rotation you must follow protocol strictly. You are released on probation and violation of this mercy will result in immediate exile and disarmament."

Duke sighed with relief and humbly nodded. "Yes sir, I understand. Thank you."

"You are dismissed." Cidolfas concluded the hearing, and everyone got up to leave. Cidolfas took Kyra back to his office. Once they got there, he closed the door behind them. "So, what do you think of your first day with the higher responsibilities of the Engineer caste?"

"I enjoyed lunch." Kyra replied with a nervous laugh.

Cidolfas laughed back. "Court was intense, wasn't it? I wish I could say it gets easier, but it does not. This is not an easy job, which is why we take those exams so seriously. We cannot take this responsibility lightly, we must make sure only the best and brightest take this role on. It's not just assembling circuits, it's applying that intelligence to the biggest problems in society. It's not just court either, we also handle city planning, we review anything the Freemen do if it would have a far-reaching impact. We don't want to restrict anyone from enjoying freedom, but we can't let anyone do anything that might actually hurt others. The clarity to make such decisions without abusing that power is a special trait. Your written exam suggests you have this clarity, and you are therefore the most fit to bear the burden. But ultimately it will be your choice, if you don't want it, you can be reassigned to another position in the bureau, making circuits and reviewing infrastructure. But also know that if you do, you will leave the job to someone less qualified, and while you will not have to bear responsibility directly, you will be indirectly responsible for allowing them to pass the decisions you were not brave enough to make yourself." He reached into a cabinet and pulled out a bottle of finely aged whiskey and poured himself a small glass. "Do you want one too?" Kyra shook her head and Cidolfas put the stopper back in the bottle. He sat down behind his desk and sipped his whiskey. "I have to be honest, that man was lucky the vote turned out the way it did. If it had fallen on me, I would have voted exile."

Chapter 5

A week had passed since the exams, and everyone was settling into their new vocations. Gol could not have been happier than working as a Smith. It was simple enough work, get some metal and an order to shape it and pound it with a hammer until it took the shape desired. It came to him so naturally he hardly even needed to think about it. Then Angus came to him with the gator skin suit.

"It took longer than expected, but Wedge finally came through." Angus proudly showed it to his apprentice. "Why don't you go try it on? Let's see how it looks on you."

"I don't know if now is a good time." Gol replied. "I have work to do."

Angus shook his head. "You've been working plenty hard, if anything, you're ahead. You can take a break for a little bit. Now go try it on." He pushed the pile of leather into Gol's hands.

Gol looked down at the clothes in his hands and then back up at Angus. "You're not going to give up until I try it on, are you?"

"Nope." Angus aid without moving at all.

With a sigh, Gol carried the clothes to a smaller room and changed. He was surprised to find that not only did it fit well, but it was also surprisingly comfortable. The outfit was slightly asymmetrical, but standard style for cyborgs, there was a glove for the right hand but as the left arm was metal already the sleeve was cut bare to expose the cybernetic. The glove and boots were gray and matched his cyberarm but were also in stark contrast to the cuirass and breeches which were reddish brown. He stepped back out to show Angus, noticing his mentor was wearing a similar outfit. "I have to admit it, this is very comfortable, but I don't know if this is practical for working in the Forge."

Angus laughed. "Of course, it's not practical for the Forge, but you're not going to be in the Forge today. You're taking the rest of the day off from Smith duties to practice fencing. I want you to make us proud at the annual tournament." He grabbed a couple of swords and Gol's clothes. "Come on we're going to the gym for practice."

Angus led Gol to the gym, a building full of rooms that were sized for sparring, just enough room for two sword wielders to duel safely. Angus held out a sword in each hand for Gol. "Choose your weapon."

Gol looked at both swords. "They look the same."

"Ideally, yes." Angus agreed. "But there are subtle differences. When you pound out the metal into its shape, it's impossible to do the same exact way twice. Even the metal you start with can vary by just the slightest in weight, density, purity. Of course, with enough skill and practice, it is possible to get them close enough that only the most experienced could notice these differences. Since I am more experienced and brought the weapons for us, I know these differences well enough that I could give you the inferior of the two blades. It is therefore customary for me to prove I'm not claiming an unfair advantage by allowing you to choose which blade you want to use so I can't rig the duel in my favor. Now choose."

Gol examined both blades as carefully as he could, but ultimately, he had no idea which was the superior blade or if there even was enough difference that it mattered. Finally, he picked up a sword and Angus readied himself with the other. Immediately, Angus shifted into a battle stance and went from a bubbly Smith to a stern warrior. "The first lesson was choosing the blade, the second is holding it. You need a good stance, it's not just about the arm holding the sword, the whole body must be balanced against it. As one hand holds the sword, the other hand remains in line behind you, the whole body should be lined up, one hundred and eighty degrees, perfectly straight, or at least as close as you can manage. Balance your weight evenly on your feet until you need to act, defense on the rear, offense on the front. But do not be too aggressive, if you give in too soon you give your opponent opportunity to dodge to the side and counterstrike. Always assume there will be a counterattack, always assume a parry, start by luring your opponent out. Get in a rhythm with your opponent and feel them out, then break the rhythm by throwing them off balance, and that is when you strike your scoring blow. As for the scoring blow, remember you are not aiming to hurt your opponent just make the contact that makes it clear that you had the advantage that you could, that scores you your point. Now, that's the basics, let's see how well you can follow these directions."

Gol mirrored Angus's stance and copied his moves as they practiced the basics of dueling. They went back and forth with Angus commenting "Good!" or "Nice!" but they seemed to accomplish no more than clashing metal like it was a dance. Gol continued to play along with Angus and for several minutes, the dance seemed to be enough for Angus. "Okay, you've got the basics, now let's mix it up a little!" Angus tried a new technique, spinning the sword around to come from a completely new angle that Gol did not expect. Gol had to improvise and parry the surprise attack. "Excellent! Now how about this?" Angus followed up with a twist that looked impossible in the second it took to execute, and Gol twisted back to block the strike. "Superb! But can you block this?" Angus thrust his sword directly toward Gol's middle and Gol desperately but successfully blocked this strike as well. "Well done! That last move was a little clumsy, but it worked well for a first timer. Now, try using those same moves against me."

Gol wasn't sure what to do, he had barely kept up countering these moves let alone copying them. He tried his best to remember what Angus did and did a rather clumsy job of echoing those techniques. His best attempt was the thrust, or at least he thought it was until Angus blocked it seemingly effortlessly. Angus tried to hide his disappointment, but Gol could see it anyway. "Okay, not bad for an amateur, but you still need work to be the best. But there is definitely potential, so we are not giving up, let's go again!"

They continued like this for an hour or so, Angus demonstrating techniques and challenging Gol to counter and copy each move. Eventually, they began to tire a little and Angus allowed for them to take a break. "You are doing well, it may not feel like it, but you are making progress already. In fact, I'd like to try teaching you an advanced style of techniques. These techniques are not great for tournaments, in fact they are restricted."

"Restricted?" Gol asked. "Do you mean they are illegal to use in tournaments?"

Angus rolled his eyes a little. "Not illegal entirely, just dangerous enough that they shouldn't be used too much or there is a penalty. Mostly to discourage powerful fighters from abusing an advantage. And to make sure you don't kill your opponent."

Gol's eyes went wide. "What kind of technique are you going to teach me?"

Angus waved his apprentice down. "Relax, I'm just talking about combat electrokinesis. You demonstrated some skill in the sewer when you took out the gator." Gol glanced down at his armor. "You used electrokinesis in a very crude but effective natural style, but there is a style of finer techniques that conduct the electricity through the metal of the blade. Actually, there are two distinct styles, one for swords and one for claws, but you won't be able to learn the claw style until you win your claw license at the tournament. For now, we will focus on the sword style. Now as I said, this is restricted because it is dangerous, but also because few have the excess charge energy to use it very often, some can't use it at all, so those who demonstrate skill in this style get promoted to their own league. But first, everyone must compete together in the beginner's tournament to establish themselves, which means following the rules that this technique sees limited use."

"If it's so restricted why teach it to me at all?" Gol asked.

"Because not everybody follows the rules." Angus answered looking Gol dead in the eye. "If you aren't prepared, they can kill you before the referee can apply the penalty. They will be disqualified, so that should deter them, but that won't make you any less dead. You have the potential to fight properly so it would be a shame if that is your end because I failed to prepare you. Now, as I was saying, the style is all about conducting your electric charge in your sword, which means you need to hold the sword with your cybernetic hand."

"But we've been holding it with the other hand." Gol said. "Wouldn't it be a dead giveaway to switch hands like that?"

Angus nodded. "Yes, that is your first hint. Most fencers hold the sword with the flesh hand, so if they switch to the cyber hand, expect that they will try electrokinesis. But knowing that it is coming is only half the battle, you also need to know the technique so that you can counter it, and to counter it, you need to be able to use it. Just like countering a sword requires you to know how to use a sword, the electricity also requires the same complementary skill set. Now, as I was saying, hold the sword with your metal hand and focus the charge to build up within your blade. Remember, the point is to channel it through the blade, so don't release it too soon. Be careful, in fact for now, don't release it at all. You only have so much energy to practice with, so don't waste it, learn to control a small amount first."

Gol held the sword in his left hand and began to build up a charge. He did have some degree of control that he had practiced before in his youth, but this was definitely new, and it took all of his focus to control the charge, for it to build up and yet remain static. His arm and sword began to glow blue and crackled with small bolts, radiating palpable energy.

"Yes, that's right." Angus encouraged him. "Now hold it carefully, don't let it go. Just see how long you can hold it, just practice that much before we test movement."

Gol continued to hold the charge but lost track of time. It could have been minutes, it could have been seconds, it could have been hours for all that he could tell. Finally, he let go, and a bolt shot from his sword.

Angus managed to deflect the burst before it caused any damage. "Okay, that's enough practice holding the charge."

"But it was only once." Gol said. "I can try again."

Angus grabbed his hand. "No, it's fine really. You did okay on the first try, but you only have so many charges in you at a time and I don't want you to waste any more energy on that when we can move on to executing and refining applied technique. Now, charge your blade again, but be ready we're going to practice dueling again."

"With electrically charged swords?" Gol asked.

"With electrically charged swords!" Angus emphatically confirmed. He charged his sword, indicating it was time for Gol to do the same. "Now be careful, when the swords are charged, it's going to have an extra kick."

Their blades clashed and just as Angus had warned, they reverberated a lot harder and knocked Gol back and he fell down. Angus laughed. "I warned you, this is why you need to train. If you go up against a particularly ruthless opponent, they won't hesitate to use that trick to take you down. If you don't want to be that ruthless yourself, it's fine, but at least be prepared to defend against it."

"But how?" Gol asked. "And why didn't you fall too?"

"Because I was ready." Angus replied. "Like I said, weight forward for offense, weight back for defense. Make sure you're grounded, hold fast but be prepared bounce back and feel the charge. You need to channel it back, just as you channel the electricity into the blade, you need to channel the electricity back from the blade and absorb it."

"That sounds like it hurts." Gol said.

"It does." Angus said. "But not as much as falling on your butt. Now let's try that again."

They tried going through it a few more times before Gol got it, and then a few more to make sure he had it right.

"You're doing good." Angus said. "Now we move on to the next higher step, projectile sword bolts."

Gol's eyes went wide. "Wait, what now?"

Angus shook his head. "Relax, it's just the same as a standard bolt, except that you channel it through the sword. You already did it, by accident, now we are going to try doing it on purpose. The hard part is defending against it, but it's just a combination of the techniques you already know. So, you have the basic skills, we know that for sure, but just because we know you have the potential, we need you to actually do it and comprehend how to repeat it. And there is only one way to do that."

"Practice." Gol said.

"Practice!" Angus repeated. He then did a few more bolts, challenging Gol to defend against them. Gol took a few bolts well, but then he started breathing heavily. "Okay, you need a break."

Gol almost argued, but he needed a moment before he could even speak. "Is it that obvious?"

"Yeah." Angus said. "It's okay, don't worry, it's just standard fatigue. You will be alright, but not if I keep pushing you. Just as you can only produce so many charges, you can also only absorb so many as well. You will recover, but at this stage of your training we have hit your limit."

"So how am I doing?" Gol asked.

"Average for a beginner to be honest." Angus answered. "That's how I can tell just by looking at you. I have seen it before, and I can gauge your well-being. Now, let's go get lunch." Angus took Gol's sword from him and set both down against the wall, then led his apprentice out of the room and down to the cafeteria.

As they approached the cafeteria, Gol recognized a familiar face. "Kat, what are you doing here?"

"The same as you, I imagine." Kat replied. "I'm training for the tournament. By the way this is my mentor, Ruby."

"That's my mentor, Angus." Gol pointed his thumb at Angus who waved in greeting to Kat. "So, you're going to be a Fencer too?"

Kat nodded. "Yes. I have been helping Hunters and sometimes the ones that need me the most need me because they are not good enough fighters for the quarry they take on, so if I want to survive, I need to pick up the slack and be prepared to defend both of us."

"Don't you have a staff and a familiar for that?" Gol asked.

Kat nodded and sighed. "And yet, it's still not enough. To be fair, it's not always the Hunters, some beasts are just exceptionally dangerous. Still, for my own safety, I'm going for my claw blade license. How about you?"

Gol shrugged. "I killed a sewer gator and now Angus here thinks I'm the next great Smith Fencer."

"Don't be so humble!" Angus said. "Gol here is the best I've seen since, well me!"

Kat couldn't resist taunting her friend. "Ha, I'll believe it when I see it."

"Hmm, not a bad idea." Angus said. 'How would you like to spar with him?"

"Wait, what?" Gol and Kat said in unison.

"You need to practice against someone your own level." Angus said. "Both of you. I already taught you the basics Gol, now you need to practice against someone with different but equal skills. What do you say Ruby? Your apprentice against mine?"

Ruby nodded. "You do have a good point, Angus. This would be an excellent training opportunity for you Kat. The best Fencers have always been Smiths and Hunters. Hunters tend to be the most practical from learning to fight wild beasts, but Smiths make the swords and know the weapons best. You'll probably learn more from studying with them than any other training I can give you."

"I guess I'm in then." Kat said.

Gol looked around at everyone, who had seemed to agree to this decision without actually asking him, but felt it was pointless to argue when it was three to one. "Okay, but can we at least get lunch? I'm starving."

"Of course!" Angus said. "Let's grab some grub!" Angus led the way into the cafeteria and directed them to get the best food for training. "You need some protein so get a quarter pound of roast poultry, and a big heaping pile of vegetable medley, with extra greens! Now for something to drink, you'll want some fresh wheatgrass juice!"

Gol looked at what was being given to him. "You lost me after poultry."

Angus laughed. "It's acquired tastes to be sure, but you'll thank me later. You can't argue with results!"

"Eat up Gol." Kat encouraged him. "Proper nutrition is key to be at your best. And especially drink your juice, it has electrolytes you need for your electrokinesis. You have been practicing that haven't you?"

"Yes, I have." Gol answered a little surprised she would know. "Have you?"

"Of course!" Kat answered. "The Order of the White Magi are some of the best electrokinetics in the land. Our style is far more defensive, but the ability to nullify electric charges is a worthy skill in combat."

Gol looked at Angus. "So why did I practice all those charges, if she can just nullify them?"

"I was trying to teach you to nullify them too." Angus replied. "But she's right, Black Sword style is more offensive, White Magi style is more defensive, she'll teach you a better style of electrokinesis for fencing."

Gol nodded. "Knowing both would make me an expert."

"I don't know if I would go that far." Angus corrected him. "But you would be more well-rounded, that's for sure. When you get into the tournament you will face many opponents with many different styles. Fencing is open, the great equalizer between castes, anybody can participate. Hunters are the most motivated because they can make the most use of the claw blade license and the practical battle experience. Smiths have our own style but it's more about pride and honor for us, so we have different reasons, different motivation, and a different style. And for the same reasons, everyone else will come in with a different style, Healers are more defensive and less aggressive, others are completely wild and jump in without knowing what they are doing and just want a chance at glory, and some of those are naturals who will develop a style out of necessity and raw talent that is unlike anything else you'll see. It's great to master our own style but knowing how to anticipate the alternative forms will make all the difference."

After lunch they returned to their training room and resumed sparring. Gol began the way Angus trained him. He couldn't go on the defensive because he knew that would be Kat's style, but he also knew her defensive style would be superior, so he had to anticipate that as he went on the offense. He leaned in with a feint to draw her into combat, and then adjusted accordingly. Her style was noticeably different than Angus. She seemed to use her sword almost like a shield, but it wasn't out of fear, she was steady and confident, clearly looking for an opening to drop a surprise strike, an opening Gol had to be careful not to give her. They went back and forth for a few rounds when Gol thought he had an opening and went for it.

Kat pulled off a surprise counter deflecting the strike and tapping him with the flat of her blade. "Gotcha! Tag you're it!"

Gol groaned and got started on round two. This time Kat was smiling and acting more playful. Gol made the mistake of thinking this meant she wasn't taking the match seriously and that he could take advantage of her lack of focus. But when he went in for the score, she once again countered, spun and struck him with the flat of her blade. "Gotcha again! Are you even trying?"

Gol grunted, took a breath and went for a third round. This time, Kat actually laughed in his face, openly mocking him and treating him as a joke. This time he was sure he could get her in a moment of weakness. He was so frustrated he threw an electric bolt at her, not too strong, just enough to stun her so he could finish the round, but she deflected it with a fluid motion that caused it to dissipate harmlessly into the ground without breaking her momentum. In stark contrast to this defensive electrokinetic technique, she moved her sword in a flimsy, clumsy fashion. He tried to thrust at her and she turned herself into a back flip and when she came up her sword was at his throat. "So close!"

Gol threw down his sword in frustration. "How do you keep doing that? It doesn't seem like you're taking this seriously and yet you keep winning?"

"Let's take a break to recover a little." Kat handed Gol a restorative potion and took a swig of one herself. "Your problem is that you assume I'm not taking this seriously because I want you to think that. I'm goofing off to distract you, but I know what I'm doing, I'm always on the defensive and prepared to counter your next attack. You are looking for moments of weakness that aren't really there, so I'm in control and that's my advantage. You need to relax and think like me."

Gol looked at Ruby. "Did you teach her that style?"

Ruby shook her head. "No, she surprised me with those skills, she's a natural."

Kat drew his attention back to her. "Remember when we were kids, and we would play in the fields? We'd pick up random sticks and pretend we were Fencers."

"That was years ago." Gol said.

"But that's where we get our muscle memory." Kat said. "It may have been play, but it was also practice. You already have skills Angus noticed, that started from our kids' games. The problem is you are trying to be a disciplined adult and still fighting against chaos. This is the beginner's tournament, so you're going to get more like me that will take advantage of you being too rigid. Now let's go again like old times." She readied her stance.

Gol picked up his sword off the ground and mirrored her. They went at it again. This time he was more casual, reading her movements, he didn't lean into her feints anymore and tried to draw her out. He started to remember their wooden sword fights. He remembered her tricks, but more importantly, he remembered his own. He decided to mix the style Angus had taught him with his own original moves. Kat noticed and kept up with the familiar techniques. Gol threw a few bolts toward Kat to test her, and she deflected each one while still keeping her focus on the duel without letting herself get distracted. Gol saw that his regular technique wasn't working so he improvised a new angle to try to catch her off guard. He almost got her, but she deflected and managed to spin around in time to deflect the sword blow he tried to complete the combo with. The fight went on for several minutes until finally they seemed to get tired. Kat appeared to be the first to falter. Gol leaned in for the score, and Kat prepared to perform her counter but to her surprise she found the sword against her throat. Gol looked Kat dead in the eye and smiled. "Gotcha!"

Chapter 6

Zeke was also preparing for the fencing tournament, but in a very unorthodox way, though common enough for Hunters, he took on jobs hunting wild beasts. Mostly he was pursuing mantises, not only were they good practice because they were dangerous, but their thick carapaces and sharp claws held high bounties and sold very well so he made pretty good money redeeming their bodies. Occasionally other beasts would challenge Zeke, but he would make the most of every opportunity. The longer he hunted, the more desperate he got, but he also got better. He wore armor made from the shells of the first mantises he had bagged and that protected him from a lot. When that didn't work, he used mantis claw daggers to finish off his quarry. When all else failed, he used restorative potions that Kat had left him.

Kat had offered to stay with Zeke herself, but he was too proud and stubborn and insisted on hunting on his own. The truth was he realized he had relied on her too much. He needed to prove himself and to do that he needed to go alone. It was exhausting, but he felt like he was improving faster not leaning on anyone.

One day he pulled his haul into the guild. Mack looked over the carcasses he had collected and rang up his bounty. "Two hundred gold for the lot."

"Two hundred?" Zeke said with shock and disappointment. "The last time I brought in a haul like this you gave me four hundred!"

Mack shrugged. "You're flooding the market, the more you bring in, the less they're worth. Try hunting some new game. Have you considered taking up another gig from the job board? It's been a while since you took a sponsored request."

"I'm trying to train for the fencing tournament." Zeke said.

Mack nodded. "Yeah, so is everyone else. If you were really serious, you would hit the gym like everyone else. But if you insist on learning the hard way, I think you might be up for a dragon's den."

Zeke perked up. "That sounds interesting. I've heard of dragons, but I don't think I've encountered one. Tell me more about this one."

"Dragons are pretty much like you've heard." Mack began to explain. "They are big lizards with wings. They spit fire more than they breathe it, they produce a highly toxic mucus that ignites when it comes into contact with air. But most importantly, they have a habit of hoarding shiny stuff in their dens. They are very protective and will hide deep in caves or dig deep burrows if they can't find a cave. Very much a nuisance since their shiny hoard tends to consist mostly of precious metals that Smiths and Engineers want. So, if you can find a dragon and hunt them to their den, you can collect quite the payday. Provided of course you survive the experience."

"Challenge accepted!" Zeke replied without hesitation. "Now, where do I go?"

Mack pointed to the board. "Take a notice, they have a map to the general area. Now that only helps you find the entrance to the den, if anyone was brave enough to map the den inside, they would have finished the job themselves."

"I got this!" Zeke said. "No problem!" Taking down a notice from the board he went out to get his silverwing and ride out to the den. Fortunately, the path was mostly empty because it went through territory that he had been clearing out lately. The beasts could smell him and knew to stay away, at least the ones that were in the area Zeke had marked by hunting. That part had overlapped with the dragon's hunting territory and there weren't many beasts that were brave enough to be out there either. The danger for the last leg of the journey wasn't the beasts, but the side of the mountain where the den was located. The dragon had been terrorizing a mine, it enjoyed collecting any shiny ores and gems the miners removed from the mine and had been ruining deliveries. The miners so far had been lucky enough that the dragon had only been collecting materials and sparing the miners themselves.

Zeke approached the cave but found that the cave opening was up on the side of a cliff. Clearly the dragon was able to access the cave by flying and was relying on how it was otherwise inaccessible to protect it. Zeke wasn't going to let something like that slow him down. His bird couldn't get up the side of the cliff, so he had to leave the bird alone at the base and find a way up on his own. He tried to find hand holds and climbing by hand alone, but he kept slipping.

"Do you need any help?" Came the voice of a stranger.

"Who are you?" Zeke asked.

The man reached out his hand in greeting. "My name's Cole, I'm a miner. I take it you're a Hunter and you are answering the posting about the dragon bounty."

Zeke took Cole's hand and shook it. "Hello Cole, I'm Zeke. How could you tell I'm a Hunter, is it that obvious?"

Cole laughed. "Nobody comes out here except miners and hunters. Nobody else has any business here. I know the miners well enough, I don't recognize you, and you're wearing armor. But the biggest hint you were here for the dragon was climbing to the dragon's den. Trust me, there's nothing else up there, so there is no other reason for anyone with any sense at all to be climbing that cliff. So, you're either a hunter that needs a little help climbing, or you're just crazy. Do you need climbing gear, or do you need me to take you to the Healer's Temple?"

"Do you have climbing gear?" Zeke asked.

"Yeah, back at the camp." Cole said. "Which you would have found if you had checked in first instead of taking the shortcut straight to the cave. Follow me, and bring your bird too, I'll watch him while you're hunting."

Zeke followed Cole and found the camp just outside the mine. There was nobody else around. "Where is everybody else?"

Cole laughed again. "In the mine of course. I'm just on guard, watching supplies and minding the carts." He ushered the silverwing into a pen.

"On guard?" Zeke asked. "From what?"

Cole laughed once again. "The dragon of course! And gremlins."

Zeke raised an eyebrow. "Gremlins? What do they want with the mines?"

Cole shrugged. "They're desperate scavengers. They will take anything if they think they can use it to survive in any way. Ever met a gremlin?"

"Only one." Zeke said. "And the encounter didn't last long."

Cole nodded knowingly. "Like I said, they are desperate scavengers. Gremlins are exiles, and that isn't taken lightly, anyone who gets sent out into the wilderness is a threat. It is a punishment that isn't taken lightly and has serious consequences, so when you encounter a gremlin, it's the worst of the worst. But one bounty at a time, let's focus on the dragon. Where did I put that climbing gear?" Cole sorted through a box. He pulled out a long rope and a few hooks. "Here you go, this will get you up to the cave. We lend this out to the Hunters that try to take this job on."

"Why is the gear still here?" Zeke asked. "What happened to the other hunters?"

"Because nobody has succeeded yet." Cole answered while adding a torch to the supplies. "Every time it seems clear a Hunter isn't coming back, we bring it down before the dragon destroys it and save it for the next guy. And I think you know what happens to the other hunters. Last chance to back out."

"I don't quit." Zeke said defiantly staring Cole dead in the eye while taking the climbing gear and the torch. Without another word, he headed back to the cliff.

"Good luck." Cole called after him. "You'll need it."

Zeke returned to the cliff and threw the grappling hook with the rope up to the ledge where the cave opening was. He used the other hooks to steady his grip on the wall while he climbed up the rope. Once he got up to the cave he started into the dragon's lair. Soon he had to light his torch as he noticed the cave went much deeper and darker than he expected. He came to a fork in the tunnel, and he wasn't sure which way to go. Then he caught a whiff of the dragon's smell down one tunnel. It was a sickeningly sour smell, like the malbur's breath but burnt. He continued down the tunnel, deeper and darker with every step.

Finally, after many twists and turns, Zeke found the dragon's den. The light reflected off from nuggets of gold, silver, copper, and iron, as well as a few gems here and there. In the shadows, he could see the silhouettes of various other objects, mostly metal tools, some cybernetics, and most disturbing of all, bones which appeared to be both cyborg and animal alike. Judging by the weapons near the cyborg remains, it seemed obvious that they were all hunters who failed. Zeke started to reconsider if this was a good idea.

Before Zeke could think about leaving, the dragon found him. It was a large reptilian creature, its body roughly the same size as a person, the neck and tail tripled its length. Its front limbs were wings rather than legs, and it had a bifurcated crest that looked like goat horns. But what concerned Zeke the most was the mouth full of sharp teeth and which could be full of fire at any moment. His first instinct was to run and hide behind a pile of ore. The dragon had spit fire at him and just barely missed. The dragon pursued, very angry with the intruder. The next blast of fire went over Zeke's head, and he rolled out of the way. As he rolled, he landed next to a corpse holding a shield and cursed himself for not thinking of bringing one himself. Then he realized that he could take this one and grabbed it before he could think about why it hadn't seemed to work for its last wielder. He held up the shield to protect himself from the next blast and noticed that could still feel the heat through the shield and almost dropped it. As he struggled to hold the shield, the dragon landed on him and tried to bite him, scratch him, and whip him with its tail. He held his shield over his face because it was the only part that wasn't armored, tried to hold the torch in the same hand as the shield to free his other hand, and drew his sword to strike at the dragon. Holding three items at once and blocking his own vision it became clear to him why this was a challenging bounty and why he should have brought a Healer or other back up. Too late now he thought to himself.

While Zeke wasn't able to strike any major blows with the dragon on top of him, he was able to hurt it enough to make it recoil and give him enough space to think about his next move. Unfortunately, that space also gave the dragon the opportunity to spit fire again. He was frustrated that the dragon had the advantage of a ranged attack, but then realized he had a way to even the field, he could use electricity. He hadn't practiced this skill, relying more on brute force with his sword, but he was familiar enough with the concept he was sure he could pull off something. He sheathed his sword and shifted his sword and torch to his right hand and charged up a bolt to throw at the dragon. It didn't work as well as he hoped, the dragon was barely phased. He tried again and again. Then he felt a buzz as he rubbed against a metal heap and figured out what the problem was, the metal was drawing away the electricity and absorbing it, so it didn't all hit the dragon.

Zeke had to stop and rethink his strategy, and while he did that, the dragon spit more fire at him. He blocked it with his shield and finally came up with an idea. He rammed the dragon with his shield, catching it off guard and slamming it into a pile of metal ore. Then he put all the charge he could muster into a point-blank shock, which incapacitated the dragon, but as the metal conducted the electricity back to Zeke, he got some of it too and both passed out for a moment.

When Zeke regained consciousness, he could not feel his left arm at all. The groggy dragon was just stirring, and its first act was to try biting him again. In its confusion it forgot what else it could do and instinctively just wanted to eat the immobile intruder. In a split second, Zeke reacted by drawing his sword and slashing the dragon in one movement. He caught the beast completely by surprise and struck a fatal blow and it fell dead next to him. Zeke breathed heavily as he moved the corpse aside. He looked around to take inventory of his haul and smiled and then laughed. Between the bounty and his share of this horde, he was rich.

Then Zeke noticed four round objects in the center of the treasure horde. It was painfully obvious what these were, dragon eggs. A few thoughts went through Zeke's head all at once, but the only one that persisted was wondering how much the eggs would be worth. He made up his mind that these would be the first things he would take with him, stuffing them in a bag he found among the other random rubbish the dragon had dragged in, the possession of another hunter who may have been better prepared, but clearly less fortunate in his attempt at slaying the dragon. He slung the bag across his back along with the shield he had used to fight the dragon and then began to drag the dragon's corpse out, knowing he would need proof. Soon he realized it was too heavy and too far, especially with his one arm not working too well, he would just take the head and throw it in the bag with the eggs.

Although Zeke had reduced the size of his immediate haul, it was still pretty heavy, but he thought about the payday he was in for and found the strength to drag his catch all the way back to the mouth of the cave. Just when he almost gave up, he saw the light of the sun peering through. He breathed a sigh of relief at the fresh air, then he began his descent down the rope to the bottom of the mountain. Another sigh of relief at reaching the ground. There was no feeling quite like coming home after completing a hunt, both the feeling of accomplishment and just the relief of survival. He began to walk back to the camp to prove his success so he could claim his reward and get his silverwing to ride home.

Cole's eyes were wide with surprise. "Well, I'll be, you actually survived! A lot of people will be mad about losing their bets in the pool. And a few will be happy, the odds were against you, but a good payday for some brave gamblers."

Zeke was almost offended, but then he remembered how many hunters died in the dragon's lair and how lucky he was to escape as narrowly as he did, so he bit his tongue and began the exchange for the reward and payment. What he received upfront wasn't a whole lot, but he knew he could get more later on when he went to scavenge the cave. After doing his business at the mining camp, he mounted his silverwing and returned to the city to check in at the guild.

"The mighty dragon slayer has returned." Mack said when he saw Zeke come through the front door. "Your arm doesn't look so good, you're going to need to rest. I can tell by the way it's hanging by your side you overdid your electroshock. But at least you made it back alive so you have a chance to recover, that was better than a lot expected. A lot of Hunters lost some money on this one."

"The miners were one thing but the guild too?" Zeke exclaimed. "You sent me on this job, why would you do that if you think I'd die?"

Mack shrugged. "It was time to sink or swim. Either you pulled it off or you were never strong enough to be one of us. But you succeeded, so did you find anything good in there?"

Zeke smiled. "The dragon had a pretty big hoard, almost enough to fill this tavern. It's going to take a few trips to collect everything, but I got a shield. I also picked up a few other things, how much are they worth?" He poured the eggs out of the bag onto the counter.

Mack's eyes went wide, his mouth went wider, and he dropped his dish rag. "Dragon eggs? Now that's something! It will take me a while to work out the deals with the merchants, but they're worth their weight in gold! Maybe more! At least three thousand here! One thousand for each egg, more if we can raise the price at auction."

"Wait, three?" Zeke asked. "I found four. Where is the other one?"

"Maybe you dropped it on your way home." Mack said. "Don't worry about it, you're going back to collect the rest of your spoils, I'm sure you'll find it out there somewhere. Really, it's not that big of a deal, you survived your first encounter with a dragon and came home with three eggs, you did good for a rookie hunter. Take the win. We're going to have dragon meat on special, the rest of the guild is going to love it. Have you ever had dragon meat? It's naturally spiced, you don't even have to marinate it."

"Yeah, I'm sure it's exquisite, I can't wait to taste it." Zeke replied. He collected his initial bounty from the guild and went on his way. It really bothered him that he lost an egg, and he couldn't get his mind off of it. He considered retracing his steps, but he looked out the window and saw the sun setting and getting too dark outside to see anything. It really was more dangerous after dark because there were nocturnal beasts that were even more dangerous than the animals that came out during the daytime. Zeke wasn't particularly afraid of those beasts, but he realized after the day he had put in, with his arm still burned out from overuse of electrogenesis, he wasn't in any shape to take them on and make it home alive. Exhausted, he ordered dinner, ate his fill and went to bed.

Chapter 7

The day of the tournament finally arrived. Gol and Kat were ready to go and arrived at the arena together. They were greeted by Kyra in a formal dress tailored to her body. "I see you're both fighting today."

"Yes, we are." Kat replied.

"Are you participating too?" Gol asked.

Kyra laughed just a little. "No, just a spectator. As an Engineer I get VIP seating. I'll be cheering you both on."

"Save some cheering for me." Zeke said as he approached. "Not that I need it, I'm gonna win!" He approached Kyra and put his arm around her. "And then when I become a professional league fencer, I'll restore my honor and we'll be together."

Kyra promptly removed Zeke's hand from her person with a look of disgust on her face. "I fear it may take more than this one tournament to restore your honor and far more than you can imagine for us to be together."

Zeke raised an eyebrow. "Have you found yourself another suitor perhaps? A prosperous Engineer at the Bureau? Tell me, who must I put down to reclaim my place?"

"It was never your place to begin with!" Kyra exclaimed. "And I haven't found anyone, I have been too busy with my duties. I have been making chips, assembling circuits, and handling administrative duties around the city. Being an Engineer is a very time-consuming vocation, not that you would know." As she said the very last words, she made sure to look Zeke directly in the eyes so he would feel the full weight of it.

Zeke did feel ashamed by her words, but his feelings for her kept him from showing his anger. He frowned for just a moment so the others could see his true colors, and then he smiled to try to hide it as best as he could. "Let's wait and see how the tournament turns out. May the best man win." He looked at Gol as he said this.

Gol was not intimidated. "Yes, may the best man win."

"Or woman." Kat added.

All three stared at Zeke so hard he could feel their eyes on him. Still, he was too stubborn to back down and instead he walked off to join the other contestants, exiting as dramatically as he possibly could.

“Is it wrong that I want to beat him just out of spite?” Gol asked.

“I hope not.” Kat replied. “Because I feel that way too.”

“That’s unsportsmanlike conduct.” Kyra reprimanded them lightly. “But he started it, so why don’t you go finish it. I’m going to take my seat, you two go and join the other competitors, the event is about to begin. Good luck my friends, may Hinu be with you.” With a polite bow, Kyra left to ascend into the audience.

Gol and Kat went off in the same direction that Zeke had gone. All of the Fencers gathered in the preparation room. There wasn’t much here, just some benches to sit down on while waiting your turn. But even the sitting and waiting would come later, right now was the opening ceremony and introductory march. Every competitor would come out in front of the audience, and they would all march around the arena for all to see who was about to compete. Everyone lined up and proceeded out a doorway that felt too narrow for everyone that had to pass through it. The march was cued up to the sound of trumpets playing the familiar music played to open every sporting event.

The Smiths all stood out in metal armor because they had the time and resources to make their own. The Hunters also stood out in their armor made from animal hides, which appeared somewhat inferior, but the exotic hides they collected were almost as tough as metal and made up the difference in flexibility and mobility. Then there were the others, the random hopefuls who had come to take a chance in the event where all entered equal, though it seemed painfully obvious from how they were dressed that they were not equal. They had hobbled together their makeshift armor from whatever they could obtain, and some were better than others. Kat fell into this last group, wearing thickly padded cloth armor that was aesthetically satisfactory by the standards of the Order of the White Magi, but while it was the best outside of the Smiths and the Hunters, it was inferior to both. Kat also stood out significantly as the only member of the Temple and would be representing them entirely for this tournament, the only Healer mixed in with the scrappers from every walk of life.

As they completed their march and stood out in the arena looking at the audience, Kyra was honored with announcing the competition. "Welcome everyone to the annual Tournament of Amateurs, the great equalizer. This is the qualifying tournament where all Fencers get their start, none of you have participated in officially sanctioned Fencing before, and this is where you will qualify for other leagues. Those who prove themselves worthy will receive their claw blade license which will allow them to upgrade their cybernetic arms to include retractable blades that will allow them to perform advanced techniques and qualify for the Master League. One champion will walk away with a grand prize of one million gold coins!" Everyone applauded with excitement, and once it died down Kyra continued. "And this year, as a special bonus, the top male and female competitor will each win a dragon's egg provided by the Hunter's Guild! Remember, these are not duels to the death, one only need bring their opponent to the point of vulnerability as determined by the judges. Once victory has been determined, the match is over, please accept the results and depart the arena for the safety of both Fencers. Aside from that, please try your best and give us all a good show! Without further ado, let the games begin!"

The crowd roared with applause as the Fencers exited the way they entered. A chart was shown determining the order of the duels. Everyone took their seats to wait their turn except the two that were first to compete. Gol and Kat sat next to each other for comfort until their matches began. Kat was extra nervous, the women were scheduled first which mean she would be the first of their circle to go in.

Gol tried to make her feel better. “You got this Kat. We have been training for a while now, and you have gotten very good. I’m sure you are going to win.”

Kat blushed a little. “Thanks. I’m sure you’ll do well too.”

“It doesn’t matter how well either of you do.” Zeke said. “I am going to win! The prize is mine!”

Before Gol or Kat could say anything, a stranger interjected. “Will you shut up already you arrogant, pompous, blowhard!”

“How dare you talk to me like that!” Zeke replied. “Do you know who I am?”

“No, should I?” The stranger replied.

“I am Zeke, the son of Chancellor Cidolfas!” Zeke exclaimed.

The stranger remained unaffected by this news. “Is that supposed to impress me? I don’t care. None of us do. Fencing is the great equalizer, everyone proves their worth in a fight. If you win, we respect you. Until you do, you’re not better than anybody else here. You’re nobody.”

Zeke was speechless. He looked at Gol and Kat, then he looked at the stranger, then back, then just gave up and stormed off. The others couldn’t help but laugh. The stranger called after Zeke. “My name is Marcus by the way, not that you care about anyone else but yourself, you spoiled brat!”

Before they could say anything else, Kat’s name was called, and it was her turn to go out and compete. Kat turned and pulled away from Gol, and they both hesitated for just a moment. As they locked eyes, they kissed quickly. “For good luck.”

The stranger approached Gol. “Is that your girlfriend?”

Gol nodded.

“Nice.” The stranger remarked. “How long?”

“Known her? My whole life.” Gol answered. “Girlfriend? Fifteen seconds.”

Everyone’s attention turned to the fight in the arena. Kat was paired off against a woman who appeared to be wearing patchwork armor. It was clear this fighter was one of the less advantaged ones, neither a Smith nor a Hunter, not any proper training, just a street scrapper looking for any opportunity she could find. For the same reasons she would be easier to fight, she would also be hard to fight, because her fighting style would be chaotic and unpredictable.

Sure enough, the other girl struck first, and Kat barely blocked the first attack because it came so quick. Before Kat could counter, the other girl came back with another strike. She relied heavily on speed, but moved too fast to have much thought or strategy behind it. The whole style was just to move so fast that her opponent couldn't counter. The problem was, one needed a lot of stamina to keep up a barrage like that, and if she didn't score a winning blow very soon, she was going to falter and leave herself open for Kat to finish her. Kat's strategy was to just wait until her opponent tired herself out. She focused on her opponent's blade and made sure to keep her own sword between her opponent and any vital parts. She had been trained in the best defensive style there was and kept up pretty well, but she knew she couldn't break concentration for a moment. Then Kat saw her opponent falter, her sword slipping down the side of Kat's and swinging out in a wide arc away from Kat. Kat saw the opportunity and thrust in to strike her opponent's chest for a winning blow. But her opponent surprised her by deflecting the blow with her metal cybernetic hand which bought enough time to bring her sword back. Kat barely registered what happened in time to block with her own metal hand. As they paused in a stalemate, she looked up at the judges, thinking this was not allowed, but they did not react. She realized there was no rule against this style of fighting, just that it wasn't standard. Kat would have to adapt.

The two fencers went back and forth for a few more rounds, Kat struggled, and her opponent appeared to have the advantage of speed and it looked like Kat was going to lose any moment. She had to watch and defend and not take any opening for granted. Her opponent was aggressive and ruthless.

Finally, Kat felt a shift in energy, they were both faltering, and they would need to end this soon. Kat knew she was reaching her limit and needed to throw everything in one last desperate finishing move. She put all her weight into a counterattack, pushing back against her opponent until they both swung their arms out wide away from each other. Kat continued with the momentum to spin full circle to strike her opponent from the other side. Her opponent could read the trajectory and prepared to block, but then Kat pulled a surprise move, then drawing her sword back to spin right past her opponent's blade and swung backhanded on the opposite side of what was expected. With a quick hard slap from the flat of Kat's blade, the match was over, a horn signaling her victory.

Kat's opponent begrudgingly held out her hand in honor and Kat took it to shake on their match. Kat was declared the winner of this match and went to sit in the winners' circle of seats to watch the remaining fights with the other victors. More women took their turns dueling in the arena, but none put on a show like Kat had, it was obvious to everyone she would win the women's division, the only question was whether she could defeat the men's champion and take the final.

Next was the first round of the men's division. Two by two, the pairs of duelists went out to fight, and Gol and Zeke waited their turns. Zeke wandered by again, impatiently waiting his turn, he resorted to his favorite hobby, taunting Gol. "It looks like Kat is going to be the women's champion. Too bad I'm going to have to take her down in the finals."

Gol remained unperturbed. "For someone who failed the Technocracy Placement Exam, you sure have a lot of confidence that fencing is your thing. I didn't even see you training at the official facilities."

"The best don't train at the gym, they train in the field." Zeke replied coldly. "I have sharpened my blade on many foes, including a dragon. Top that!"

"The one Kat fought looked to have been trained like you." Gol replied. "Just taking opportunities to develop her skill however she could. That didn't cut it for her, and I doubt it will cut it for you."

"I guess we'll find out in the ring." Zeke huffed.

"I guess we will." Gol agreed. It wasn't long after that it was Gol's turn and he entered the arena with sword in hand, ready to fight. Gol looked into the audience to see both Kyra and Kat cheering him on. He appreciated both of his friends, but he found Kat's support seemed to mean more to him. He couldn't let his mind be distracted though, fencing required concentration, especially the foe he was facing now.

Gol's opponent appeared to be a Hunter, wearing leather armor with reinforced plates made from the bones and shells of the animals he had fought. It was efficient armor and intimidating because its strongest points were trophies from his victories in battle. But most intimidating of all, Gol recognized this fighter from the gym, he had been preparing with professional training and knew a specific Hunter style.

Gol's first strategy was to take a defensive stance so he could learn to read his opponent's style and hoped he would be aggressive so that he could take advantage of that momentum. Sure enough, the man started off with a bum rush. Gol defended against the attack with all he had, putting all his weight into pushing back with his sword to guard against this attack. Gol pushed back so hard his opponent actually stumbled backward from the recoil. They went back and forth like this for a while, it became clear his opponent relied on brute force over skill. Gol just needed to find an opening, but it was hard because each strike was a wide arc that drove his defensive blade away from the weak spot that would have opened. Gol could not seem to find an opening that he could take advantage of without leaving himself open.

Gol tried using an electric attack to stun his opponent to throw him off. Gol didn't like having to use a technique like that, but his guilt turned to a different kind of regret as his opponent deflected the shock blast. The man laughed and suggested that the bar had just been raised in the worst way possible. He charged up his blade with electricity and Gol realized he needed to generate a complimentary charge to cancel that out or he was going to get knocked out by the electricity alone. They kept this up for about a dozen blows before they were worn out and had to return to fighting without electricity, but it was close, just one missed charged strike and either one could have fallen on the spot. As it was, they could both barely move their cybernetic arms having worn out their electrogenic muscles, they hung by their left side while they fought strictly one-handed.

Finally, Gol figured his opponent out. He waited until his opponent was recoiling from a strike and preparing his next move. Right at the turning point between moves when it was too late for him to change direction, Gol swayed to dodge rather than block and counter. Gol spun with his opponent's momentum to swing and slash at his torso and landing the blow with the flat of his blade. A horn signaled Gol's victory and the two shook hands honorably.

Gol looked back to the audience again and saw Kat with her arms wide open to welcome him to the winner's circle. Gol reciprocated her embrace, and they took their seats next to each other. They felt more at ease after their first round knowing they had qualified for their claw blade license and could just relax and watch the rest of the round as spectators. The next few matches were certainly more entertaining without them needing to worry about their place.

The skill level varied a lot after Kat and Gol had taken their turns, but it did seem like they were going to be the top two. Still the others did offer some impressive competition and the day was very entertaining. Finally, after everyone else, Zeke was one of the final two competitors of the first round. His opponent was Marcus, the same guy who had interrupted him earlier. Zeke hadn't taken the time to learn his name, but he had time to develop a grudge.

As they went into battle, Zeke lunged for the first strike. Just as before, the first strike wasn't necessarily the best move, starting defensively gave Marcus a chance to read him and prepare. Zeke's aggressive approach made it seem like he had the advantage at first, but to the fighters who could understand what they were watching, it was obvious that Marcus had the upper hand. He was parrying every strike with little effort. He was just waiting for Zeke to wear himself down.

Zeke began to slow down and faltered just a little bit. Marcus saw the opening and tried to take advantage of it. It turned out to be a trap, Zeke countered, parrying Marcus's attack and striking back. Marcus just barely dodged in time, pulling back just in time to avoid the losing blow. They went back and forth like this for a few more rounds. Zeke continued to be aggressive and didn't seem to have any strategy other than to wear Marcus down and try to take advantage of moments of weakness. The problem was that seemed to be the same strategy they were both employing, so it was a matter of who could use this tactic better and who had more stamina.

They hacked and slashed, and bobbed and weaved, all around the arena. They ended up hitting the walls a lot, both with their swords and with their bodies, sometimes with their heads. Every crash got a loud reaction from the crowd, some cheers, some groans, but all excited. This was definitely the longest, most active, and most interesting and entertaining fight so far. Metal clashed against metal and the thunder rang through the arena, louder with each hit. At one point they even resorted to kicking each other. Two kicks and Zeke was thrown against the wall. He heard the crowd cheer as he hit the wall, then he rolled out of the way just before Marcus got him and the crowd booed. It was in that moment that Zeke realized that everybody was rooting for him to lose. He had believed this was his moment to prove himself and earn everyone's adoration, but it quickly looked like that wasn't going to happen. Then he felt the flat of his Marcus's blade smack him and realized in that one moment he was distracted, he had lost.

The world seemed to slow to a stop as Zeke watched Marcus raise his hands in acceptance of the cheers and adoration. "The cheers and adoration that were meant for me!" Zeke thought. Zeke picked up his sword and went to take another stab at his opponent.

"Look out!" Kyra screamed.

Marcus couldn't turn around fast enough to avoid the attack, he had dropped his guard now that the official sanctioned duel was over. Not only was he open and vulnerable, but Zeke wasn't just playing anymore. The crowd gasped together as they saw Zeke's blade emerge from a bloody wound. Marcus fell while Zeke stood triumphant. He looked out at the crowd too blinded by rage to see the horror on their faces to see what he had done. Fencing was a sport, nobody was supposed to get hurt, let alone killed. The whole arena went silent as they all stared at Zeke, his whole body heaving from the deep breaths he was taking, looking like a madman.

Kat ran to Marcus and Ruby came down from the stands to help her take care of the patient. They examined the wounds. "His vital organs are fine, just some minor damage to his liver. If we can stop the bleeding, he might be okay." They proceeded to stitch the wounds closed and wrap them up with bandages.

"Zeke!" Cidolfas exclaimed. "Look what you've done! You have violated the sanctity of our favorite sport. You have committed murder. We have managed to avoid a crime like this for so long, I can't even remember when it last happened. To ruin that record, to bring bloodshed in a sport meant to channel such urges in a more civil manner, that was horrific enough, but to know it was you..." Cidolfas's voice trailed off as he hung his head in shame, but then he found his voice again. "I trusted you to find your place in this world even when I knew better. Zeke, when you failed the exam, the council reviewed your results and made a determination about you, one that I rejected, because I thought you deserved a chance, but you squandered that and now I can protect you no longer. For the crime of murder, you are to be exiled."

Zeke laughed maniacally, then raised his sword to point it at Cidolfas. "And how do you think you can stop me, old man?"

The other fencers came out of the stands and pointed their swords at Zeke. He saw that he was outnumbered and halted. Cidolfas came forth with Gol following close. "Drop your sword." Zeke did as he was told, but begrudgingly so. "Gol, please hold Zeke for me."

Zeke's eyes went wide. "No! Please, no! Don't do this to me father!"

"I am your father no more!" Cidolfas exclaimed. "You have disgraced my family, you have disgraced my legacy, you have disgraced the entire Technocracy!" He took Zeke's cybernetic arm and pulled it from his flesh. Zeke screamed in pain, but nobody felt sympathy for him. "Go now to the wilderness, and never return. You get nothing but the clothes on your back. Join the gremlins who have turned their back on us as you have. You are not welcome here anymore."

The other fencers prodded Zeke out of the Arena when he refused to leave of his own volition. They continued to chase him through the streets until he was out in the woods. They stopped at the edge of civilization and watched him until he realized there was no going back for him, and he had to travel out into the wilderness alone.

Meanwhile back at the arena, Cidolfas concluded the event. "Due to unfortunate circumstances, we will not continue the tournament. All the first-round champions will receive their claw blade licenses. As for the grand prizes, the judges scores will be reviewed for how well everyone did in the one fight they participated in, the high scores we determine will receive the appropriate prizes. We thank all fencers for your participation and the audience for bearing witness to the better matches of the day. Go home safely."

With the crowd leaving, the professionals had time to handle the pressing matter of the dying fencer. Ruby called for help transporting her patient. "We need to get him back to the Temple. He might make it but only just barely."

"Do we have medicine to help him?" Kat asked.

Ruby sighed. "I don't know yet, I need to check what we have in stock, but it will be easier to determine once we get there." Gol helped carry Marcus out of the arena. Kat and Ruby took turns using electrokinesis to attempt to stabilize him, but he was visibly struggling. He was barely breathing when they got him to the Temple, and he was put in a bed in the infirmary. Ruby started grabbing bottles and jars from the shelves and mixing whatever she could to apply to the wound, though some medicine was administered orally. Kat continued to apply electrotherapy. Marcus continued to sweat and cough, his wound swelling and turning horrible shades of colors Gol and Kat had never seen in flesh before. Finally, Ruby stopped and told Kat to take a break.

"Is he going to pull through?" Gol asked.

Ruby shook her head, then shrugged. "He is stable for now, but I fear he will have a hard time recovering from this. At this point, the only thing I can think of is phoenix down."

"Phoenix down?" Kat asked. "But can we even get that?"

"That is a good question." Ruby asked. "We ran out a long time ago and there is only one place where we can obtain such medicine from, and it so dangerous, even the best Hunters rarely go to collect it even though we have a standing bounty for it."

"What is phoenix down?" Gol asked.

"The most powerful medicine in the world." Kat answered. "It can heal even the most fatal of wounds. It is shed by the phoenix, a bird that lives in fire from the Sunset Mountains at the edge of the world. They nest in the heat to incubate their eggs, but to survive that heat themselves, they need an incredible rate of regeneration and most of that is in their feathers, at least the part we can harvest anyway. But the area is so hot and hostile, almost nothing else can survive there, not even cyborgs like us. Even the best Hunters don't feel it's worth pursuing."

"So, that means we have to get some ourselves?" Gol asked.

Both Ruby and Kat were a bit shocked. "We? You want to go on this quest?"

Gol nodded. "I can't just let this man die. We may not know him, but we know who did this. We can't just let this happen. Besides, I can't let you go alone Kat."

Kat nodded. "I know the way, we'll go together."

"You can start first thing in the morning." Ruby said.

"Will he be able to wait?" Gol asked.

"It doesn't matter." Ruby answered. "You two won't make it without rest. It's late, it's dark, the road is dangerous, and you two have had an exhausting day. I will not lose two people to save one, it's bad enough that you will undertake this task as it is, you at least need proper energy. Off to bed, both of you."

Meanwhile, out in the wilderness, Zeke finally found the dragon egg he had lost. He reached out to pick it up and as he touched it, it started to crack. He happened upon it just as it was hatching. The little winged lizard poked his head out and looked Zeke in the eye. Zeke understood enough about animals to know that the hatchling would imprint him as if they were family and that a pet dragon could be a good thing to have. "Well, little guy, I guess it's you and me."

Chapter 8

The next morning, Gol and Kat were awakened by Angus. "I heard you were going on a dangerous quest, and I worked all through the night to make your upgraded cyberarms with blades. You'll need them for this quest, it's dangerous enough as it is. Come with me and Ruby and I will help with the installation."

"Do we have enough time for that?" Gol asked as he was getting out of bed.

"First getting a good night's sleep, now this." Kat added as she entered from her room. "It's like you don't want us to go."

Angus dismissed the notion. "it's a noble cause to be sure, yes we want you to go. But you need a good breakfast, and you can eat while we complete the installation."

Gol and Kat conceded and followed Angus to a room usually reserved for operations and treatments. There were two chairs, one for each youth, each between two small tables. The table to the left of each chair had a cybernetic arm and the tools for removal and reinstallation. The chairs were surprisingly comfortable. "We'll just give you a local anesthetic to make this easier on you. Just focus on anything but looking at what we're doing." Angus and Ruby both applied a syringe and hypodermic needle to Gol's and Kat's left arms and proceeded to remove the cybernetic arms that had fused with their flesh over the last few months. Fortunately, they had not grown into their cybernetics too much and the removal was relatively easy. That was the hard part, and once that was done, they started putting the new arms on. It was a testament to how used to their vocations they were that they could stomach undergoing this operation like it was an ordinary routine.

Everybody finished around the same time. "All set, good to go. The anesthetic will still take time to wear off, but you should be good before you reach any dangerous territory."

Gol gave his cyber blades a test run releasing the blades and then retracting them, first all at once, then one at a time. "That works well. Thanks. We should be ready to go."

They were served breakfast now that their operations were over. Orange juice, coffee, a banana, a hash brown and an egg, cheese, and bacon biscuit sandwich. "Eat up, you'll need your strength for the road ahead." Ruby encouraged them.

"How is the patient doing?" Kat asked as they walked out to their silverwings to mount up and leave.

"Fine for now." Ruby replied. "But I'm not sure for how long. We'll do our best to sustain him until you get back, but we don't have time for any further preparations."

"All right, we'll hurry." Kat said as she got on her bird and directed Gol to follow her.

As Gol got on his bird, he noticed an extra passenger. "Kewpie? Did you follow me all the way here? I don't think you can come along on this quest."

"Actually, mole-bats can sniff out phoenixes, and they are remarkably resilient in that habitat." Kat said. "He might be useful, almost as much as my carbuncle."

"Oh, are we going to have a competition to see who has the best pet?" Gol asked.

"My carbuncle is not a pet!" Kat replied. "She is my sacred familiar!"

"Do you hear that Kewpie?" Gol said to his mole-bat. "They think they're better than us. But we'll show them, won't we?"

Kat rolled her eyes. "Whatever, let's go already!"

Gol and Kat began their journey to the western horizon. They took the main road that had been largely established just for acquiring the phoenix down. For the first leg there were a lot of farmers and merchants, but the closer they got to their destination, the more abandoned and ruined the road was. They certainly didn't have time for sight-seeing, so they just rushed through the villages lining the road. Before they knew it, they were running across an open stretch of land, with nothing to see but the road and open fields on either side for nearly an hour. Then came the forest, creeping over the horizon almost swallowing the road, but the path still cut through clearly enough they would know where to go as long as they didn't stray at all.

Kewpie whimpered, they had never been this far from civilization before, their family farm was within the settled rural region, this was far beyond anywhere they had ever traveled well into no man's land. The trees were full of wildlife making all sorts of noises, from bird tweets in the canopy, to chirps and barks from the animals closer to the ground and the occasional growl from a predator trying to decide if the travelers were worthwhile prey. Kewpie held tight to Gol's stomach while Carbuncle tried to be braver but sat in the same position relative to Kat.

Fortunately, none of the beasts seemed to be brave enough to attack the travelers and they got through the forest rather uneventfully. But the hard part of the journey had not even begun, the next leg involved a deep chasm spanned by an old bridge that hadn't been repaired in years, but still looked like it might be stable enough to cross. To avoid taking any chances that the bridge might collapse, they each dismounted and slowly walked their birds across one at a time. They made the mistake of looking down and saw just how far down the river was beneath them, far enough they could barely see it or the ground around it, mostly shrouded in darkness in the shadows of the canyon walls. Though there were some missing planks that made holes in the bridge, and it swayed in the light wind blowing through, but with careful stepping, they made it to the other side.

On the other side of the bridge things got even worse. As they went past the last few feet of the forest, the plants stopped rather abruptly. The grass and other herbs and weeds barely went a few steps beyond the edge of the forest which itself had not gone that far beyond the bridge. Looking out farther, all they saw was a flat dry desert, so hot from the midday sun that the air wavered before their eyes.

"Are you sure about this?" Gol asked.

Kat nodded. "The phoenixes nest in the mountains across the desert. The only way to get what we need is to cross this hot desert and enter the mountains."

"Is it at least cooler in the mountains?" Gol asked.

"No." Kat said, shaking her head. "The mountains are actually the source of the heat."

"Why would the birds live there?" Gol asked.

"They are adapted to the heat." Kat answered. "It's actually comfortable to them. They get cold if they leave the desert, so mostly they stay in this range and eat whatever they can find. Mostly they scavenge from anything unlucky enough to die in the desert."

"Like us." Gol said.

"We'll be fine." Kat said. "We just need to move quickly, which means the silverwings will need a rest before we sprint across the hot sand." They dismounted the birds to let them rest and took a break themselves. The Order of the White Magi had packed up their birds with rations for their journey and Kat unpacked what she thought they needed at the moment, starting with water for themselves and their birds. The silverwings grazed on wild greens while Kewpie and the carbuncle foraged for nuts, fruits, and seeds along the edge of the woods. While they ate their lunch, Kat looked up in the sky observing the noon day sun hanging high above. She looked out over the horizon and squinted hard to see if she could find what she was looking for. After a few minutes, she determined that she did see her goal. "It looks like at this rate we should reach the mountains around sunset, which is perfect, because that's when the phoenixes are supposed to be most active, meaning they will shed their down and there will be fresh material to collect."

"But then, how will we get back in the dark?" Gol asked.

Kat groaned. "We'll have to camp in the mountains. I heard that the Hunters set up a camp site there once, I don't know what shape it's in now, but we won't have much choice." After they finished eating, Kat pulled a small potion from each silverwing's saddle bag, handed one to Gol and directed him to feed it to their birds. They hopped up on their birds as the potion started to take effect. "Put your cyberhand on the bird and release the gentlest charge you can. You just want to give him enough to activate the accelerator potion in their system and motivate them. You don't want to hurt him, and you don't want to burn yourself out either. Like this."

Kat's silverwing's eyes went wide and it let out a squawk before she started sprinting across the desert. Gol followed suit and their speed was faster than they ever had experienced as the birds kicked up sand in their wake. As they sprinted the mountains came up over the horizon and got ever closer. A fiery orange line seemed to define the boundary between the mountains and the sky. The mountains did indeed seem to be on fire. Gol was surprised at how fast they were approaching the mountains. He could feel himself running out of electric charge and wondered how tired his bird was getting. Just when he felt like they were at their breaking point, they hit the shadow of the mountains and were close to the foot of the range.

"Stop!" Kat called to Gol while she took her hand off of her silverwing, indicating he should do the same. The birds slowed down and came to a stop just as they reached the mountain itself. Kat looked around and found a cave that was decorated with sigils of the Order of the White Magi. "This must be the camp. Healers that came with Hunters set this up and marked the site. We can tie up the birds to these posts here so they can stay put and rest after the run. Not only are they tired, but they won't be able to climb, so we'll have to finish this journey on foot and come back for them on the return trip."

"I'm a little tired myself, should we rest?" Gol asked.

Kat handed him a small potion, one he recognized from fencing training, the one that restores electricity. She took a swig of hers. "Bottoms up. We can rest after we get the phoenix down."

"I know we're in a rush to get this medicine, but you seem to be on a pretty specific schedule." Gol said. "Is there something you're not telling me?"

"You'll see when we get there." Kat said with a mischievous wink. Grabbing her staff, she began leading the way through the back of the cave to rear exit out to the mountain trail with her carbuncle following behind. Zeke grabbed his sword just in case and followed with Kewpie bringing up the rear, scared but not wanting to be left behind. The rear of the cave went down to a hot spring with a rusty metal bridge going across it. Gol was a bit skeptical of another bridge, but Kat was confident enough to go across. Gol followed of and found that it was more stable than he thought.

After the bridge, the mountain trail was considerably more stable and reliable, provided that they remained on the trail. To either side were sharp rocks that appeared very menacing. In between the cracks, steam and smoke seemed to pour out. The higher they went, the more steam and smoke came out from the ground and the more frequent the small geysers as boiling liquid erupted from the ground. "This place seems very dangerous."

"It's a volcano." Kat said. "That's why there's a desert out there, this mountain emits so much heat that it has boiled the land dry."

"Why in the name of Hinu do phoenixes nest here?" Gol asked.

"They are well adapted and don't mind the heat." Kat answered. "And besides, it keeps away predators, so it's the safest place for them to be."

"Yeah, I can't imagine anything would want to live in a place like this." Gol said.

"Well, there is one thing we may have to watch out for." Kat said. "Salamanders. They are the only other creatures that can stand this heat and share the habitat. Fortunately for the phoenixes, they tend to prefer lower elevations, so they don't bother each other very often. Unfortunately, that means their habitat is between the ground and our destination."

"You mean right about where we are right now?" Gol asked.

"Yes." Kat answered. "Keep your eyes peeled."

"Why didn't you mention this before?" Gol asked.

Kat shrugged. "I didn't really think about it, kind of taking the journey one step at a time."

"Are you sure we're going to be okay?" Gol asked.

"Yeah, we'll be fine." Kat replied. "Just look out for salamanders."

Just at that moment, Kewpie stopped sniffing a steam vent and ran back to Gol being chased by what appeared to be a little lizard that was on fire. Gol killed it quickly. "I take it that was one."

"Yes." Kat replied. "But they can get bigger."

"How much bigger?" Gol asked. As if on cue, three larger salamanders crawled out of the walls onto the path ahead, each roughly the same size as a person. They spit burning hot spit at the travelers, which the carbuncle managed to block by emitting a strange energy bubble from the gem in her head. Kat swung her staff while releasing an electric charge that parted the flames on the nearest salamander just enough for her to make contact with a fatal blow to the head. Gol attacked another salamander using his sword and an electric charge that wasn't nearly as elegant as Kat's approach, but still effective. Gol and Kat came together with their cyberblades to finish off the last one before it could react. "Yeah, those are pretty big."

"Actually, I've heard they can get even bigger." Kat said.

"How much bigger?" Gol asked.

"Probably twice as big as those ones." Kat said. "Maybe three or four times as large, but not more than that. The good news is, I've heard there's only one of those at any given time, the alpha guardian of the territory. For some reason the others stay at the size we just saw until the alpha dies and then another will grow to take its place."

"Probably because the big one eats the others." Gol guessed.

Kat shrugged. "Nobody has stuck around long enough to find out."

Just then they came up to a large hot spring, and this one was red and appeared to be completely boiling, much hotter than the first one they had seen earlier. The first one had merely felt hot, but this one was bubbling with steam rising in thick clouds. Gol looked at it. "I'm just going to take a guess that this is where the alpha salamander lives."

Kat scanned the area. "Probably. We might want to be careful and quiet as we work our way around it."

Gol looked at Kewpie. "This will not end well, will it?" Kewpie shook his head back in agreement. Both sighed and continued to walk slowly around the edge of the hot spring. Kat went around the other side of the spring hoping they could move faster if they didn't restrict themselves to going single file along one side. They made it halfway across when they saw something move in the pool of water and a massive head emerged. "Kat! Look out!"

Kat threw herself to the side just before the giant salamander attacked her. She smacked it with her staff while her carbuncle sunk her teeth and her claws into the beast. The salamander howled and flames emerged from its mouth and nostrils that spread down its body. Kat and her carbuncle managed to pull back before the fire could burn them.

Across the pool, Gol tried to think of what to do. The salamander was too far to hit with any physical weapon he had, so he threw an electric bolt at it. It didn't seem to hurt too much, but it did successfully draw its attention so that it turned around and came for him. It submerged back into the water putting out the flames while releasing steam. Gol and Kewpie ran for the other side. The salamander had kept its head near the surface to watch them moving and followed them to emerge just in time to cut them off before they could escape its territory. Gol struck it with his sword just before it burst into flames again.

Kat ran around the edge to assist. She realized she couldn't hit the fiery body, but she could hit the part of the salamander that was still submerged and not ablaze. The salamander howled in pain and turned to attack Kat. Gol took advantage of the moment to run to the end of pool. He reached out for Kat's hand. "Let's run!"

Kat shook her head. "We can't. The phoenixes are too near, if we run, we'll just draw the salamander into their territory. We must finish this here first."

Gol groaned and motioned for everyone to back up. "Stand back." Kewpie scampered to hide behind Kat. The carbuncle was braver, but only slightly. As the salamander lunged at Gol, he dodged to the side at the last moment and slashed at it at the same time. The blade went through the salamander's head slaying it on the spot. Gol turned back to his companions. "Are you all okay?"

The three nodded in reply. Kat turned to look ahead on the trail. "Thanks Gol, we're almost there. I can see the peak, so next is the phoenix nesting ground. No more challenges, just one last walk."

"I have heard that before." Gol replied, sheathing his sword and retracting his cyberblades. "I will believe you when we're done and safe at home."

Kat frowned with disappointment, but then conceded after she considered what they had been through so far. "Fair enough, but let's go." She turned and led the way up past the last outcropping of rocks to find the nesting ground of the phoenixes. It got much hotter as they got closer, almost unbearably so, but it was worth the sight that they beheld.

At the mountain peak was the caldera full of molten lava but above it flew a flock of phoenixes that appeared to glow like they were on fire like the salamanders, but upon closer inspection, the flames were merely an illusion of their shimmering feathers. The fiery looking birds were flying in from their daily hunt looking like rays of light breaking off from the sun as it set behind them. As the sun set the night sky became filled with a vermillion aurora, and despite nightfall it looked as if the world was on fire. Gol, Kat, Kewpie, and the carbuncle stared in awe with mouths agape, it was one of the most beautiful sights they had ever seen in their life, and with the deadly caldera below, it was also the most terrifying at the same time.

The birds settled down to roost along the edge of the caldera and the light seemed to flow down them like fire dropping from the sky. It even looked like tiny embers were falling from the living flames, until they realized these were the feathers they had come for. As soon as this fact hit Kat, she started gathering as much of the molted feathers as she could and directed the others to help her as she handed out bags to them. “Come on, let’s make this trip worth it, get all that you can carry!” She stuffed her bag full and so did Gol, with Kewpie and the carbuncle pushing feathers into piles to help stuff them into bags too.

While gathering feathers, Kat noticed an egg by itself. She looked around and saw that all of the birds seemed to have returned to their nests to claim their eggs, which could only mean that this egg belonged to a bird that didn’t make it back. After another quick look around, Kat stuffed the egg into her bag, buried in the padding of a few inches of the softest feathers in the world.

They tied a bag of feathers each to Kewpie and the carbuncle, then tied a bag each on to their own backs and carried a bag in each hand and carrying as much as possible, they began their descent back to the base camp. The return trip was uneventful compared to the trip up the mountain, ending with them returning to the cave to find their birds waiting calmly, having slept the whole time, exhausted from their run across the desert. Kat put together some dinner from the rations they still had left, dinner well earned from their climb.

After their meal, Kat went back to the spring just outside the cave. “I’m going to take a dip in the spring. I heard it’s supposed to be one of the most restorative experiences in the world. I know I need it after today, how about you?”

“Yeah, but are you comfortable with that?” Gol asked.

Kat laughed. “What, us being naked in the water together? We’ve known each other since we were kids, this isn’t even the first time we’ve bathed together.”

"But the last time was a long time ago." Gol pointed out, blushing more than could be blamed on the heat. "Before we grew up so much. We were much smaller then."

"Come on." Kat pleaded again with a smile. "Don't be so shy." She walked off to the spring and took off her shoes and then her robe. Without any hesitation, she stepped into the hot spring, taking her time and letting Gol see her. She was a beautiful woman, much more obvious without the baggy robe obscuring her figure. She was not fat nor skinny, with just the right curves. She looked back at Gol as she submerged almost up to her shoulders. "The water is perfect."

Gol pulled off his gator leather armor and waded into the water as well, taking notice that Kat was eyeing him and saw him as much as he had seen her. His body was as well shaped as hers, but in a different way. He had grown up working on the farm and since he left the farm, he had spent just about every day either swinging a hammer in the forge or a sword at the gym and his muscles showed the results of all that exercise.

Kat smiled looking at her handsome companion. "How does it feel?"

"Good." Gol said. He found himself at a loss for words.

Kat came closer when she realized Gol had stopped. "Here let me massage your muscles. As a Healer it's my job to make my companions feel better. You feel so tense, but I guess that's understandable after the last couple of days we've had."

"Are you sure this is the right time for this?" Gol asked. "A man's life is hanging in the balance."

"And it won't do him any good if we try to rush home and get ourselves killed by nocturnal beasts." Kat countered. "So, we might as well relax and enjoy ourselves. We almost died multiple times today alone, how much longer are we going to put off talking about our feelings? I know our parents were hoping you would be with either me or Kyra, and honestly, I always hoped it would be me that you would choose. I thought when we kissed yesterday, you were finally ready to make up your mind."

"I am." Gol said. "I did. I do...love you. I always have."

"Then what's wrong?" Kat said, rising from the water a bit more, baring her chest, daring him to look at her.

"I don't know." Gol said. "I guess, it's just that...I saw the way other guys treated you and Kyra, guys like Zeke. I don't want to be like that."

Kat put her hand on Gol's face. "You're not like him. I know you better than that. It's okay for you to be honest with me."

"And you're sure this isn't moving too fast?" Gol said.

Kat laughed. "For as long as we've known each other I think if anything we're going too slow. We should make up for lost time."

Gol and Kat kissed and then got out of the spring and moved to the cave for the rest of the night.

Chapter 8

"Good morning." Kat said to Gol as he woke up the next morning. She was making breakfast. Half of their remaining rations, they were going to have to make it back home soon, not only for their patient, but for their own well-being. Their silverwings were even more well rested than their riders were, and they were ready to go.

However, as they stepped outside the cave, they were greeted by a bizarre sight, four cactus plants that were in vaguely human shape blocking their way. "I don't remember these being here yesterday."

"They weren't." Kat pushed Gol back out of the way back into the cave and the cactus plants moved and shot their needles at the travelers. "Those are cactruns. Unlike normal cactus plants, they can move and are very violent and territorial. Not much is known about them except that they are fast, they throw their needles, and they are deadly enough that most people run away before they can learn anything else."

"And the ones that don't run?" Gol asked.

"They die." Kat answered.

"Well, how do we run when they are blocking our way?" Gol asked.

Kat thought for a moment. "How strong is your electrokinesis?"

"Do you think that will stop them?" Gol asked.

"Stop them?" Kat echoed, shaking her head. "No, but it should distract them and slow them down enough for us to run past them."

"Okay, good enough." Gol said.

"Okay, but just one more thing." Kat added. "I have two more accelerators for our birds for the return trip, let's give them their drinks so that they can move faster, and we can make our escape. My carbuncle can give us some cover and I'm going to give you a mana potion because you're probably going to need it after you take on the cactruns."

“That sounds like something for all of us.” Gol said. “But what about Kewpie? Do you have any plans for what he should do?”

“Yeah.” Kat nodded. “Hold on tight.”

They jumped on their birds, gave them their potions and Gol charged up his arm to release a blast on the cactruns as he exited the cave. The plants dodged the bolt, which Gol had never seen before, but when they dodged, they parted to leave an opening for the travelers to escape through. They immediately rushed with the carbuncle projecting an energy field behind them to repel needles if they were chased.

And they were chased. The cactruns moved faster than anything Gol or Kat had ever seen, and they even seemed to move faster than their silverwings. The needles came fast and hard and the carbuncle’s defense barely held until the barrage ended. A few needles got through and poked everybody resulting in shrieks of pain from everyone involved.

“Okay that’s it!” Gol screamed. “I don’t care how dangerous they are, they are about to find out how dangerous I can be!” He drew his sword and slashed at the nearest cactrun cutting it in half. Then he swung his sword the other way and took out another cactrun on his other side. The other two started to pull back. “Oh no you don’t!” Gol released his cyberblades and crossed them with his sword and charged up all the blades at once through the point of contact, then slashed toward the cactruns releasing a powerful cross bolt that took out both cactruns at once. “That should keep them away!” Gol took a swig of his mana potion and put his hand on his silverwing and they triggered their sprint back to the edge of the desert.

Once they made it out of the desert, they stopped to eat the last of their rations and rest up for the last leg of their trip. From there, the remainder of their trip was rather uneventful. They just hoped they could get back in time to help Marcus.

They made it back to the Temple in the mid-afternoon and Kat burst in through the front door. "We made it back! How is Marcus? We aren't too late, are we?"

"Marcus is still alive but just barely holding on." Ruby replied. "Come quickly."

Ruby led Kat to the room where Marcus was being kept. Healers were gathered around him taking turns healing him as best as they could, trying to keep him stable until better treatment could reach him, and now that it had they parted for Kat to finish what they started. Kat had trained enough to know how this would work and ran over to him, reaching into her bag for feathers and spread a handful on his wounds. After distributing the feathers, she placed her cyber hand just an inch above the wound and gave the lightest charge she could manage, and then raised the charge just a little to activate the feathers. The feathers burned and melted over the wound as it closed. Kat was so nervous she held her breath waiting to see if it was working. Several tense seconds passed that felt like forever before Marcus finally breathed and proved he was still alive. Everyone finally sighed with relief.

"What happened?" Marcus said coughing.

"You almost died." Kat replied. "But we found a way to save you."

Marcus smiled. "Thank you." He closed his eyes.

"He needs his rest." Ruby said. "Even with the phoenix down, he has been through a lot and needs a lot of recovery time. Let's give him the time he needs, and in the meantime, we can inventory the phoenix down."

Ruby led Kat and her companions to the apothecary where they kept their medicines. Together they found a place to store the feathers and proceeded to unload the feathers from the bags into the new containers while Ruby took note of how much they collected. "You got quite a lot, this should help a lot of people if anything bad ever happens again, Hinu forbid." As they got to the last bag, Ruby found what else Kat had collected. "What's this?"

Kat blushed a little with shame, she knew it wasn't something they were supposed to do. "I took a phoenix egg. It was the only one without a parent, I didn't know what was going to happen to it left on its own, so I brought it back."

Rub sighed and paused in thought before saying anything. Gol interrupted during the awkward silence. "Did we do something wrong?"

Ruby finally shook her head. "The phoenix is a sacred bird, and they thrive in a unique environment, we are not supposed to try taking them out of their habitat. However, since this one has already been removed, there is something else we can do under special circumstances we are lucky to be experiencing at the moment. We are going to put this bird in the menagerie where it can be incubated with the dragons."

"Dragons?" Kat and Gol said in unison.

"Yes." Ruby smiled, happy to share some good news with the youths. "You two were determined the winners of the fencing tournament and each received an egg, and I would like to ask that you put them in the Menagerie. Once they hatch, they will be able to produce fire that will help make a suitable habitat for the phoenix. The Beastmaster Guild already prepared the habitat at the menagerie for the dragons, there should be enough room for the phoenix, at least as a hatchling, and this will give them enough time to figure out something better long term."

Kat sighed with relief and her blush receded. "That's great news! Of course, I'll offer up my dragon to help the phoenix! How about you Gol?"

Gol was still taken by surprise. "Of course, I'll turn over my dragon. What was I going to do with it? Kewpie and my silverwing are enough animals under my care, I don't need a third."

"Actually, you may still be involved in raising the dragon and regular care." Ruby said. "The Beastmasters tend to animals at the Menagerie, and provide them with a home, but in the case of animals donated by individuals such as yourselves, you are allowed to come and help. They actually need the help, the guild doesn't make much money on their own and mostly rely on volunteers to get anything done."

"Still, I don't have any room to raise a dragon." Zeke said. "So I'm in."

"Very well." Ruby replied. "Come with me." Ruby led them to the Menagerie, which was on the edge of the city. Kat recognized the area, this was where she had come with Zeke when they responded to the bounty from Zamas on her pet, Carrot the malbur. In fact, when they got there, they were among the first they encountered. They were in a pit designed to resemble the bogs malburs normally inhabited and keep the malburs from getting out or even close enough to hurt anybody outside the enclosure.

"Hello there!" Zamas greeted them as she was tending to Carrot in his habitat. "You're the one who helped me bring my Carrot home. Kat, right?"

Kat nodded. "Zamas, how are you doing?"

"I'm doing quite well dear." Zamas replied. "After Carrot got away, I realized I couldn't risk it happening again, so I turned to the Beastmaster Guild to house him in the Menagerie. He still doesn't like anyone else but me, so I come in to check on him and give him his regular care. How about you?"

"Turning in some beasts of my own." Kat answered.

"Isn't that lovely?" Zamas commented. "And who's with you? That doesn't look like Zeke."

Kat shook her head. "No, he's not Zeke, this is Gol, and he's my boyfriend." She grabbed his arm and locked elbows with him with a big smile.

"More good news!" Zamas replied. "I'm so happy for you. It sounds like things are going well for you."

"We must be running along." Ruby reminded Kat. "Those eggs won't get themselves to the hatchery."

Kat waved to Zamas. "Have a nice day!"

"You too, dear!" Zamas replied as she turned back to Carrot.

As the group continued through the park, they saw a number of animals in enclosed habitats similar in size to the malbur's enclosure but modified to meet the needs of the animals inside. They saw wolves, tigers, bears, and even a mantis in forest style habitats and birds in large cages that kept them from flying away but still gave them enough room to be comfortable. Lizards sunned themselves on rocks in a miniature desert while scorpions scattered around them. There was a large pool that was filled with fish, mollusks and crustaceans of all shapes and sizes, some partitioned off to prevent them from eating their neighbors. There was one particularly large enclosure for a behemoth, the largest beast anyone knew of, much larger than a dragon even. The behemoth was huge, each limb was bigger than a person, its massive horned head looked like it could swallow someone whole in one bite.

Then there was another eye-catching exhibit, a forest habitat that was home to what appeared to be children, but they were naked except for thick fur covering them from head to toe and they were swinging around up in the trees by their three limbs. Something about their faces didn't look quite right either, these were not cyborgs, yet eerily similar in appearance.

"What are those?" Zeke asked.

"Gremlins." Ruby answered.

"I thought gremlins were people that were exiled." Kat said confused.

Ruby sighed. "That's a derogatory term for exiles yes, but the term comes from true gremlins, which are these wild beasts. They are believed to be related to us, which is why they look so similar, but they do not have the ability to speak and are not capable of understanding any part of civilization. But the one thing that makes them remarkably similar to cyborgs is that they have the same electrogenic organ in their short arm stump and seem to be the only other species capable of electrokinesis. But they were hunted nearly to extinction. They still live on islands to the south, but on the mainland the only ones left are in the Menagerie."

"Wow." Gol and Kat said in unison.

"But enough distractions, we really need to get these eggs to the hatchery!" Ruby reminded them.

The group got moving to their final destination, a building in the back of the Menagerie that kept smaller animals like rats and spiders. Deep inside this building in the back was the nursery where orphaned wild animals were brought to receive care and be raised to settle in their proper homes. This included the hatchery where eggs were brought and it's where they found another familiar face.

"Kyra!" Gol and Kat said in unison as they embraced their friend.

Kyra gladly returned their hug. "Kat, Gol, what are you doing here?"

"We could ask you the same thing." Kat replied. "We're here to hatch eggs, two dragon eggs that we won in the fencing tournament and a phoenix egg we found recently." Kat proudly presented her eggs.

"I also have a dragon egg." Kyra replied presenting hers. "Three came in all at once, the Hunter's Guild was auctioning them off. Two were claimed by the Fencer's committee as prizes and the third was gifted to me."

"Who gave it to you?" Kat asked.

Kyra furrowed her brow. "Strangely, I still haven't figured that out. But here I am, with my egg, and I have no idea what to do with it, so I'm trusting the Beastmasters to help me out."

A woman entered the room. "Sorry to keep you waiting. Some of these animals are very high maintenance, but every one of them is precious. Anyway, I'm Willow leader of the Beastmaster Guild, pleased to meet you all. I understand we have some dragon eggs to hatch."

"And a phoenix!" Kat proudly held up her egg.

Willow's eyes went wide. "Interesting! Well, I'd be worried about a phoenix egg under any other circumstances, but with three dragon eggs, I am less concerned and more excited. Phoenixes need fire or their eggs won't hatch without sufficient heat. But dragons can breathe fire, which means if we surround the phoenix egg with the dragon eggs, that will help keep the phoenix egg warm, and when the dragons hatch, they will instinctively breathe fire and that heat should be enough to help the phoenix to hatch. We can keep all four together and their combined heat will help all of them grow."

"And you aren't worried they'll eat each other?" Gol asked.

Willow shook her head. "No, dragons aren't cannibalistic, and phoenixes are strong enough to survive dragons when they are the same age and size. The dragon's primary advantage would be fire, but the phoenix is one of the few species that won't work on, so they'll be fine. Now come along."

Willow directed them to the incubator, a large metal bowl, built into a stand fixed to the ground, filled with straw. First, she took the phoenix egg and placed it in the center of the nest, then she took the dragon eggs and placed them around the phoenix egg, equidistant from each other.

"Now what?" Gol asked.

"Now each of you step right in front of your egg and put your cybernetic hand on the metal edge of the incubator." Willow directed Gol, Kat, and Kyra. "Start slowly channeling a light electric charge, the eggs are sitting on plates connected to the edges so it will conduct the heat to help the eggs hatch."

Gol, Kat, and Kyra did as they were told. It took a while, but eventually the eggs start to shake and crack open, and the little winged lizards emerged. The first thing each dragon did was approach the cyborg that hatched them and nudge their hands.

"The hatchlings have imprinted on you." Willow said. "From now on they will see you as their parents. You'll appreciate that when they get bigger. Would you care to name them?"

"Leviathan." Kat replied without hesitation.

"Syldra." Kyra said with a surprising smile on her face. "They're so cute when they're little."

Gol stared in thought for a moment. "Bahamut."

"All good names." Willow approved. "Now all we have to do is wait for them to work on the phoenix egg."

The dragons then turned to look back at the last egg in their nest. They approached the egg and sniffed it, then poked it with their snouts, and then started breathing fire at it. First, they all breathed fire at it at once, then they took turns for a little while, and then finally all at once again. The last time caught the straw on fire, and they all got startled and jumped back, gliding back to their cyborg parents.

"Don't worry, it's okay!" Willow reassured them. "That fire will help the phoenix, let it take its course."

The fire continued to burn around the egg, but it didn't seem to be damaged at all. The fire grew more intense, seeming to consume the egg, but still the egg itself did not seem to be harmed. The fire continued to grow intense, feeding on the egg like it was some sort of candle melting slowly and evenly all around at the same time. Then something strange began to happen, the flames went from the shape of the egg to the shape of a bird uncurling, the egg had hatched, and the bird was now emerging in fire. The flames died down slowly and even more subtle because the bird's plumage so closely resembled fire that even when it stopped burning it still looked like it was on fire, shimmering feathers colored vermillion and golden, it took a few minutes to realize the whole thing was over.

"That was amazing!" Willow said. "I've never actually seen that in person, but that was certainly something. Now let's take them to their habitat." Willow led them to another room in the back of the building. The room had a large cage that extended outside the building and was exposed to the open air while keeping the animals inside. The ground resembled the rocky desert mountains where they found the phoenix. There was a large mound in the middle with three large holes in it. "The cage will keep them from flying away, but they have enough space to move around, get exercise and grow. Those holes will serve as their dens when they get older and bigger, and the phoenix will nest at the top of the mound. We will provide them with food, water, and treasure to satisfy their hoarding needs and they in turn should cover the fire needs of the phoenix. This place will be safe for them and safe for us as well." Willow opened a door in the cage, and they put the hatchlings inside. The hatchlings began to scurry around their new home with childish curiosity. "Well, they seem happy enough. It's getting late now, I have had a long day, and I imagine all of you have as well, so if you don't mind, I think it's time we had all be getting home."

Gol yawned. "Yeah, I am definitely tired and ready to sleep in my own bed."

"Me too." Kat agreed.

"I guess we'll be going then." Kyra said.

They all walked back to the entrance of the Menagerie and parted ways from there. Kyra gave her friends a parting hug before departing for her home near the Bureau.

Gol walked Kat back to the Temple, but as they got closer to the Forge, Kat got a little hesitant. "Actually, I was wondering if I could come home with you. We did spend last night together, it felt nice, I think I'd feel lonely tonight."

Gol looked back at Kat, thoughtfully. "I guess if I'm being honest, I'd feel a little lonely without you too."

They kissed and then walked home hand in hand.

Chapter 9

Zeke wandered out into the wilderness with only a dragon hatchling for companionship. The tiny lizard crawled on the stump of his left arm onto his shoulder and looped her tail around the stump of his arm. “I suppose I’ll have to give you a name, won’t I? What name sounds good to you? How about Tiamat?” The little lizard gave a squeal that sounded like a pitiful attempt at a roar. Zeke couldn’t help but laugh at this. “Tiamat it is. Now, what do we do about food and shelter? Shelter isn’t looking like it’s going to be resolved anytime too soon. But food, well, I’m hungry, we’re going to have to find something.”

Zeke looked around and tried to remember what was edible. Suddenly he wished he had done more than just hunt, he had no idea what do for food when he had no weapons and no money. He saw herbs and mushrooms, but he suddenly couldn’t be sure which were edible, and which were poisonous, but he did know some were deadly and he didn’t want to take any chances.

The more he wandered, the more confused he got, until he realized why exile was so bad. He started to wonder how any exiles survived. Then he remembered the gremlins. So far, he had only seen one and he killed that one, but he knew there had to be others. He wasn’t sure now whether that would be good or bad. Worse, he had no idea how he would find one either way, the last time was purely by chance.

Darkness fell and it started getting colder, not a lot colder, but it sure felt that way to Zeke. He was getting lost and had no idea where he was now. He had to stop moving because he couldn’t see anymore. Then came the sounds of the nocturnal beasts, the legendary monsters that made the creatures of the day seem tame by comparison. He had no idea what to expect, he had never been out after dark outside of the city before. His heart started to race, he had to admit he was terrified.

Then came the eyes, glowing in the dark. He blinked and they were there upon him, and he feared this was how it was all going to end. And then one came close. "New exile, huh?"

"Yes." Zeke nodded.

"I'm Colt." The stranger flipped up his goggles and stuck out his hand. "I'm one of the newer ones, only been out here a few weeks. Or a few months maybe, you tend to lose track of time out here, ha! Oh, and you got a dragon too. What are your names?"

"I'm Zeke and this is Tiamat. I just ended up out here today, and she just hatched."

"And what got you exiled?" Colt asked.

"I murdered someone." Zeke said. "Or at least fatally wounded him, it all happened so fast, I don't know how things ended up for him."

Colt whistled. "Well, I can't judge, I was exiled for attempted murder, and if they hadn't caught me, I most definitely would be in the same situation. Actually, I guess I am. Well, anyway, you're a gremlin now, come join the community."

Zeke got up and followed his new friend to join the group of one-armed outcasts. They all looked inhuman, malnourished and disfigured by the harsh elements. And yet, they seemed to be surviving better than anyone had given them credit for. In truth, exile was supposed to be a death sentence, nobody was even expected to survive at all without modern technology, every gremlin was a feral abomination that was beyond understanding. And now Zeke was one of them.

They made their home deep in a swamp. Far beyond where any civilized folks dare tread, there were small huts that seemed to blend in with the trees. Colt presented his home to Zeke. "This is our village. It's not much, but it's what we could build from scratch. And with only one hand each."

"Did it ever occur to anyone to build in teams and each contribute a hand?" Zeke asked.

"Yes, and this is still the best we could do." Colt replied. "Starting civilization over from the ground up is a lot harder than you think. We have no tools, so we have to build everything with our bare hands, well, hand." Colt laughed wildly as he held up just one hand.

It was at this time that Zeke noticed that everyone was wearing clothing that looked old, worn, and undoubtedly the last thing they wore when they were exiled. Then there were the older and younger gremlins that were wearing animal pelts. "What's with the furs?"

Colt shrugged. "We have no needles to sew, nor looms to weave, so all we have to wear are animal skins that already the right shape."

"Why only the older and younger gremlins?" Zeke asked.

"Older gremlins wear pelts when their clothes wear out." Colt answered. "As for the younger gremlins, those are the ones that were born out here."

"Wait, gremlins have kids out here?" Zeke asked. "How are you able to survive long enough for that to happen? I thought we just struggled until we die out here?"

"Struggle until we die." Colt echoed. "That sounds right, it's just a matter of how long that struggle lasts. And some of us last a lot longer than you think we will. Long enough that we start families and thrive for generations."

"And you just stay out here?" Zeke asked. "Nobody ever tries to go back?"

Everybody laughed at Zeke. When the laughter died down, Colt answered Zeke. "Why would we go back? They have made it clear we have no place in their world. They cast us out, they will not forgive us, and they will not let us back. Why even bother trying?"

"But what about the children?" Zeke asked. "Why don't you at least send them back? They could be safer in civilization."

"Safer without their parents?" Colt asked. "Safer as orphans, living in a world that hates their parents? Safer in a world that will hate them just as much when they take after their parents and inevitably make the same mistakes? No, there is no return from exile. But that does not mean that there is no hope, just not the world we knew. There is another way."

"Is there any chance that other way could involve technology that's better than sticks and stones?" Zeke asked.

"The Technocracy keeps everything to themselves." Colt answered. "Although we do have some great minds. I was working on some new technology that broke the Taboo. If I hadn't been exiled, I might have accomplished great things. But we don't have the right materials to work with. We can't build anything without access to the right materials. All the metal is in the mines and the mines belong to the Technocracy."

Zeke stopped to think. He looked at his dragon. "Wait, not all the metal is in the mines. Dragons collect metal for their nests. They attack miners and merchants on the road. If we can find dragons, we can collect the metal from their nests. Some metal they collect is raw ore, but sometimes they also collect metal objects that have been fully shaped. If we can collect some weapons and tools, and maybe the cybernetics of those who fell prey, we could get ourselves in shape to build some other better tech, build our own city, one without Taboo so we can do anything we want."

Everybody was in awe. Colt smiled "I like the way you think! But do you think you can take on a dragon?"

"I already did not too long ago." Zeke said. "There might be some stuff still there at the den. Let's go back and collect any scraps that may be left. It'd be a start."

Colt's smile went wider. "With half as many arms, we'll need twice as many men to carry that loot, but I think I can scrape together a salvage crew that's ready for this job!"

They spent the next few hours rallying up as many gremlins as they could to go back to the cave where Zeke had slain a dragon a few weeks earlier. Soon the largest raiding party of one-armed outcasts ever assembled were heading back toward the dragon's lair. They would have been more cautious about going near the mines, but it was night and miners probably wouldn't be there. Their sheer numbers frightened off the beasts of the night who had learned that the strong smell of unbathed swamp dwellers meant more trouble than it was worth hunting.

When they reached the mountain, there were now stairs built into the side of the cliff to help with retrieval of the treasure so nobody would have to climb by rope and struggle with carrying anything at the same time. Zeke went first because he knew what he was looking for and where to find it. The others followed him as well in single file to fit in the tunnels.

When they got to the dragon's den, they found that most of it had already been removed, but not all of it. The efforts to loot this hoard had been managed primarily by Zeke, although Hunters and miners, and some other opportunistic salvagers had been helping, but the miners and Hunters had other work and salvagers found the distance to be a bit of a deterrent, so the collection had gone slower. Zeke' crew was now much more focused on getting this job done since they had bigger plans than simply making a living, they were going to build an empire. There were still a few cybernetic arms left in the cave and they started attaching the arms to try making themselves whole so they could carry more loot. Of course, Zeke made sure he got one first, then picked up one of the last swords for his personal trophies and began directing all the others to collect everything they could. Meanwhile, Tiamat was sniffing around the cave, clearly recognizing a familiar smell, and Zeke was glad he had prioritized removing the dragon remains so that it wouldn't upset his new pet.

Enough people had come along that they were able to carry everything that remained in the cave in one trip. They went home smiling with a load of metal that they could begin working the next day. They needed rest after the night's haul.

Zeke could hardly rest though. He was tired but with a new arm and a new sword and some raw ore, he had plans for the future and for the first time in quite a while, he actually looked forward to what he was going to do tomorrow.

He was the first to wake up in the morning and began his work, crafting a makeshift forge around a fire and banging metal together until he was able to fashion a hammer, then using that hammer to shape the other piece of metal into a better hammer. The clanging awoke the rest of the village, and he handed one hammer to the first aspiring smith to meet him, and they began work on more hammers, until every gremlin with two hands was wielding a hammer. Next, they were working on making more arms for more gremlins, and any who didn't show crafting aptitude went hunting and foraging for food.

As night fell, they started running low on material. Zeke led another raid, this time on the mine itself. The miners had collected more than they could bring back to the city, so they left some overnight. Zeke led his raiding party to collect all the scrap they could muster. This night they were less lucky, a dragon attacked them, wanting to steal their treasure. Zeke was undaunted, he directed his party to retreat until the dragon collected as much as it could carry and started to fly away. Zeke then led his party after the dragon, following it back to its den. Once back at the dragon's den, he directed some of his party to distract the beast while he killed it in much the same manner as he had killed his first dragon, but now more efficiently. He was quick and ruthless, and they went home with even more ore and a feast of dragon meat as well.

Zeke continued this process over and over again. He collected more metal to build more arms, more tools, and more forges. The more workers he had, the more gremlins he could make whole and the more work that could be done overall. As days passed, the wood huts became brick houses, the village grew into a city, and they began to develop other forms of technology. In time, they even began to explore forbidden technologies of the great Taboo.

Zeke held court as an emperor, directing everyone as he would have as an Engineer. He had a palace built, large, ornate, and imposing. He had the palace built on the edge of the swamp, where the land was solid, and everyone could see it's shadow looming over them and know he was watching over all his subjects. They went looking for new materials to make new things, some baubles to decorate his palace others were more practical and more important, but everything was bigger and better than anything in the Technocracy, by order of Emperor Zeke.

Zeke's favorite part of his job was hearing ideas from those who had been exiled for breaking the Great Taboo so that he could approve production of the things that had been forbidden by the Technocracy. This had always been his dream, to make the impossible things possible. The first to present an idea was his friend Colt. "Greetings, and what do you have to present?"

Colt held up a hollow metal rod. "I call it a gun."

Part 2

Chapter 10

Years had passed since Zeke's exile, and those living in the Technocracy had all but forgotten him. They had all gotten into the routine of their vocations, settled into the security of the everyday. Gol and Kat reunited with Kyra most days at the Menagerie checking on their dragons which had grown much larger but were surprisingly docile living in captivity. Whatever free time Gol and Kat had left they spent with each other and cherished every moment whether it was a dinner at a restaurant, or sparring to train for a fencing tournament, or watching the silverwing races as they were doing this day.

"So, who do you have your money on in this race?" Kat asked as they settled into their seats.

"I've got a good feeling about Teioh." Gol said. "I placed a good bet on him to win."

"Will it be enough to cover dinner after the race?" Kat asked while snuggling up to her beau.

"And then some." Gol answered.

"Well then, this bird better win!" Kat cheered.

Just then the trumpets blared signaling the race was about to begin. The announcer came along with a megaphone. "Ladies and gentlemen, welcome to today's races! The silverwings and their riders have taken their places and are ready to begin. Without further ado, let the races begin!"

With the sound of another trumpet, the starting gates opened and the silverwings began to run around the track. Everybody started cheering and shouting and screaming as the birds sprinted by. There were a dozen racers on the track, all competing to be first in line. As they came around the curve in the track, they nearly collided with each other as a few tried to pull ahead and a few fell behind. At the straight away they sprinted as best as they could and tried to switch places, reclaiming their lead, shifting again at the next turn. The whole way, Gol and Kat were watching the bird called Teioh as he led and fell back, but always remained at the front of the pack. As they came into the home stretch, Teioh was in second place.

"Come on, come on!" Gol screamed.

As they came closer to the finish line, Teioh managed to pull ahead just in time to win the race.

"Yes!" Gol cheered.

"I hope that means you're going to buy me a really nice dinner!" Kat said to Gol.

"The nicest in all the Technocracy!" Gol confirmed with a kiss.

"Good, I'm starving." Kat said with a smile.

After the races, Gol took Kat to a nice dinner at the finest restaurant in the city. Between Gol being a Smith and both of them being champion Fencers, they were making great money and could afford the finest of everything. They didn't always spend their money so frivolously, but knowing they had that money made their lives easier. Gol ordered a fine bottle of wine, followed by a nice steak dinner for each of them.

Kat raised her glass to Gol's. "To Teioh!"

"To Teioh!" Gol agreed. "This is the life isn't it, Kat?"

Kat smiled. "I know I've got all I need with you."

"Me too." Gol agreed. "Who would have thought that two humble kids from a farm would get this far?"

"I always had faith." Kat replied with a wink before taking another sip of wine.

Gol cocked his head almost in disbelief. "Actually, you always did seem to be the most relaxed of the three of us. Why haven't you ever worried about the way our life was going to go?"

Kat set her glass down. "Because I always knew you were crafty enough to become a Smith and Kyra was smart enough to become an Engineer. I had my future figured out for a long time too, it was you two who were worried you had a long shot. But maybe it was because you guys were so worried that you were so driven. But hey, we made it, so it was worth it!"

"True, life is good!" Gol said. "I really can't think of anything that could make life better. Well, maybe one thing." Gol got down on one knee and pulled out a ring. "Kat, will you make me the happiest man in the whole Technocracy and marry me?"

Kat slapped her hands against her mouth in shock. "Yes!" She put out her right hand and Gol placed the ring on her finger. "It's beautiful! It's perfect! Thank you! I love you!" She threw herself into a hug on Gol so hard he fell backward and gave him a big kiss. Everyone around them applauded and cheered.

"Thanks everybody!" Gol said as he got up and back in his chair. "Wow, everybody really seems happy for us."

"Of course, they are, we're the most well-known couple in the Technocracy!" Kat said. "You're the top Fencer in the Electric Dual Blade League and I'm the top woman in the Rod and Blade League, which is smaller, and less impressive by comparison, but I'm still number one and I have a growing fan base that has made my league the second most popular! But anyway, the point is we got fans and they want to see us happy together."

"Hold on a moment." Gol said. "It sounded for a moment there like you're a little jealous of me."

Kat huffed. "Gol, I chose to practice a different style that I knew I was better at and that's why I'm in a different league, which I knew was less popular, but I made it work. Just like I made it work when I failed the exam and found my calling as a Healer. I am where I am meant to be in my life and the next step is snag my trophy husband. So, let's get talking about this wedding, because our fans are going to want this to go big. I mean, this needs to be the biggest party of the year!"

"Why does it have to be so big?" Gol asked.

"Because we can afford to make it big!" Kat said. "Now, I'll need a dress, but that's something I should talk with Kyra about, so you and I just need to worry about venue, menu and a cake. Well, decorations and who's invited, but we really need to know where we're holding it, so we know how much room we have to work with."

"I was assuming the wedding would be at your temple." Gol said.

"Yes, perfect for the ceremony." Kat said. "But what about the reception? I was thinking maybe something around the Menagerie."

"You were thinking about the Menagerie?" Gol repeated. "How long were you thinking about this? I just asked you to marry me."

"Oh Gol, my sweet boy." Kat giggled. "I have been dreaming of our wedding since we were kids. It wasn't just our parents that thought we would end up together. They were expecting us to take over the farm, but I had higher ambitions for us, but still, we could agree that I was meant for you, and you were meant for me. I just needed to wait for you to catch up to me." As she looked into Gol's eyes, he was shocked, but she did not waver in the slightest and continued on her train of thought. "So, do you think this place caters? They do have the best food and wine in the city. But what about cake? They have good deserts here I'm sure, but we'll have to check in with all the bakeries to make sure we get the best of the best!"

"What have I done?" Gol said.

Kat laughed. "Too much all at once? It's okay, we don't have to go through all of this at once."

Gol sighed with relief. "I love you."

"I love you too." Kat replied with an air kiss.

Gol looked out the window behind Kat and saw the sunset. "Isn't that beautiful? It reminds me of that first night we fell in love."

Kat turned to look. "Memories." As she turned back to Gol, she briefly looked through another window on the North side of the building. Gol, what's going on that way?"

Gol looked up and saw a large shadow roll down towards the city. "I have no idea. I have never seen anything like that." Gol squinted and as the shadow got closer, he was able to make out a few details, enough that he started to get scared. "I think someone is invading the city."

"Invading?" Kat asked. "But who? Nobody invades anywhere. Except gremlins, but they never come to the city."

"They're coming now!" Gol said as he grabbed her hand and led her away to safety.

"Wait." Kat said. "Why are we running away?"

"Because we need to escape the invading horde." Gol answered.

"And where are we going to escape to?" Kat replied. "The only people who know how to fight are Hunters and Fencers. And we are Fencers which means if we run away, we are leaving people defenseless."

Gol paused in thought for a second. "Are you saying you want to fight them?"

Kat extended her cyber blade as her answer and without another word, she ran towards the attacking gremlins.

"Hinu help us both." Gol said as he followed Kat into the fray with his cyber blade extended as well.

Everybody else was running away from the invaders, right now only two were going against that flow and they had to be careful not to hurt civilians with their cyber blades on their way through the crowd. But soon enough they came across the invaders and it was not what they expected. Rather than one armed savages, they were uniformed soldiers with cyber blades and unfamiliar weapons that were advanced beyond anything available in the Technocracy.

As Gol and Kat approached the soldiers, the soldiers shot at them. Kat pushed Gol out of the line of fire while deflecting the bullets with a defensive electric field that diverted them magnetically just enough to miss by an inch.

"What are those?" Kat asked.

"Guns." Gol answered. "I heard a while back a Smith worked on a prototype, but the Council of Engineers stopped the project. They must have exiled the inventor and he figured out some way to resume his work outside the Technocracy. We have to be careful, those projectiles could kill us and it would probably only take one hit."

"Like arrows, but smaller." Kat surmised.

Gol nodded. "And harder to see." They leaned back against the wall and waited for the soldiers to move closer. As soon as they noticed them coming around the corner, they released bolts of electricity to incapacitate them. Or at least, that was the plan, it didn't work because their armor protected them. Gol and Kat had to act quickly to improvise, releasing their cyberblades to cut them down quickly. They ran before the next wave could catch up. "They must be wearing armor with rubber coating to deflect electricity. Whoever is in charge of this thought of everything. We need to retreat and regroup."

"We have to get to the Bureau and warn the Engineers!" Kat said. "Kyra doesn't have combat experience, I'm not sure any of them do. We have to protect her!"

Gol simply nodded as they tried to run through the streets. Running toward the invasion had been a mistake, now they were everywhere and at every other turn, the invaders were ahead of Gol and Kat and they had to either fight or turn and run another way. The city was being overrun by soldiers in every direction and the only things that were keeping Gol and Kat going was adrenaline and pure luck.

The run to the Bureau was exhausting and seemed to both go by in a blur and take forever. Once they made it to the Bureau, they ran inside and climbed up the stairs to Kyra's office. Kyra was shocked by her friends bursting in out of breath. "What's going on?"

"Gremlins are raiding the city!" Gol answered. "But somehow they got a hold of cyberarms. And other technology we've never seen."

"But how did they get that technology?" Kyra asked. "I didn't think they had anything when they got exiled."

"Somehow they figured out a way to rebuild society from scratch." Kat surmised.

A shadow fell on the window as some bizarre new unknown object eclipsed the building. It appeared to be an enormous, long, egg-shaped balloon with some sort of carriage hanging underneath.

"What is that?" Kyra asked.

As if in answer, a rope ladder fell out of the carriage and an imposing figure descended to enter the room through the window. He wore black armor, polished to a smooth shine, except for his left arm which had the same silver chrome typical of cyborgs. He wore a sword on his hip, visible under an ornate cape flowing in the breeze. He stepped forward slowly, intimidating the three stunned people. He removed his helmet to reveal his face.

"Zeke?!" Gol, Kat, and Kyra said in unison.

"That's Emperor Zeke now!" He replied with resounding authority. "After I was cast out with the other rejects, I learned that they, like myself, had potential that was being wasted under Technocratic authority. I gathered them and we rebuilt our arms from scrap and then built all that which was forbidden by the Engineers, such as this airship."

Kyra recognized it now, remembering what Cidolfas had shown her. That one had been incomplete, but now a fully functional version was in front of her. "So that's what it looks like when it's complete."

"If you think it's impressive on the outside, wait until you see the inside." Zeke said as he approached Kyra with a hand outstretched.

Kyra recoiled from his advance. "No, I will go nowhere with you."

Zeke's face soured. "I believe there has been a misunderstanding. I'm not asking, I am the Emperor, I get what I want, and I want you to come with me, now come my Empress."

As Zeke approached more aggressively, Gol stepped forward with blades drawn. "You heard her grace, leave her be!"

Zeke sneered, then laughed. "You wish to fight for her honor? Then let us fight!" He extended his cyberblades and drew his other blade from its sheath. The other blade wasn't a normal sword, the hilt was a gun affixed so that when the trigger was pulled it would release the shot along the blade and intensify every blow. Crossing the blades, he struck out at Gol. Kat intervened to assist Gol, blocking the attack from one side so that Gol could block from the other and neither attack could land. "Impressive but let's see how long you can keep this up."

The three began a battle that appeared to be a dance of blades, with every attack from Zeke, Gol and Kat parried with flawless coordination. It was as if Zeke was fighting one opponent with four arms. Somehow Zeke was able to keep up the pace without failing even being outnumbered. Kyra took advantage of the moment to try running away, but just as she made it out the door, Zeke caught her out of the corner of his eye. "Oh no you don't!" Zeke said as he turned to chase her out of the room. Gol and Kat pursued as well. As their chase went down the stairs, Gol jumped over the railing and landed on the next flight between Zeke and Kyra. Gol engaged Zeke to try and give Kyra more time to get away. "Run!"

Kat directed Kyra down the stairs while also trying to maintain a last line of defense against Zeke. As she looked back, she saw Gol holding up well against Zeke alone. They were continuing to duel and it looked as if Zeke was getting the upper hand on Gol, but every time it looked like it was over, Gol managed to make a comeback just in time. As Kat and Kyra neared the bottom of the stairs, Zeke got desperate and jumped over the railing. He grabbed the wall with one hand using his cyberclaws to slow and direct his descent to break his fall. Gol desperately followed suit jumping down the stairs, gripping Zeke's claw marks, stumbling down the wall and tumbling through the air. As Gol reached the bottom of the stairs, he desperately struck out at Zeke to try to keep his attention off Kyra and Kat. Zeke turned around and fought back, but the fall had left them both a little disoriented giving the women time to put some more distance between them. The disorientation faded for both in an instant of clashing blades as Gol blocked what would have been a fatal slash from Zeke just an inch away from death.

"You aren't strong enough to stop me Gol." Zeke said as their blades were locked. "You stole victory from me before but this time, Kyra will be mine as she was always meant to be!"

"The fact that she is running from you would suggest she is not interested." Gol replied as he continued to struggle to hold off Zeke's blade. "How did you get this strong in exile? And where did you get the new arm? None of this makes sense."

Zeke sneered at Gol as he leaned closer. "You think exile meant going without, but all we needed was a leader to reclaim what was taken from us. I couldn't rule in the Technocracy, so I made my own Empire!" Zeke pushed back against Gol with all his might and sent him crashing into the wall. Zeke turned and chased after Kyra once again. "Come here my dear!" Zeke said as he reached out to take a hold of Kyra.

"No! Get your hand off her!" Kat screamed as she desperately lashed out at Zeke. Her movement was so quick Zeke didn't see it, she didn't even realize what she had done. Suddenly blood sprayed from Zeke's shoulder as his right arm dropped to the ground between him and Kyra, still holding his gunblade. They all looked at Kat's cyberblade dripping with Zeke's blood, and a few seconds felt like an eternity as they realized she had been so determined to protect her friend that she had released it while she was reaching and severed Zeke's good arm. Kat was torn between the guilt of wounding an old acquaintance and the pride of protecting her dearest friend. She shook the blood off the blade and moved to shield Kyra with her eyes still locked on Zeke.

Zeke grabbed his own shoulder trying to stop as much bleeding as he could, but quickly realized he was outnumbered and in his current state he stood little to no chance to win this fight. He had been overconfident and now he would pay the price. He looked over his enemies who had once been friends, and then he settled on the only option he had left, to just walk out the front door alone.

Gol noticed Zeke's eyeline on the door and raised his blade to Zeke's neck. "You're not getting away that easily. You will pay for your crimes."

Zeke laughed. "What do you mean? Will I be exiled? I will simply return to my empire and come back stronger again!"

"No." Kyra interrupted. "You will not be exiled. You will be imprisoned."

Gol looked at Kyra with shock. "Is that even something the Technocracy does?"

"Is there even a prison to put him in?" Kat followed up.

"There is an old dungeon deep underground." Zeke said. "But they haven't been used in living memory. They filled up too fast in a darker time of chaos and caring for prisoners was too costly and risky for the guards. It was believed exiling cripples was more efficient."

"But clearly too merciful." Kyra said. "You cannot be allowed to be free to run your empire and threaten the Technocracy."

Zeke sneered. "Next you'll tell me I will be executed."

"I will leave that for the High Council to decide." Kyra said coldly.

Zeke was surprised. "You always struck me as kinder than that. Has serving in the government broken you so easily?"

Kyra shook her head. "No. It's just you. I know you too well, better than I ever wanted to. You have pursued me and harassed me for as long as we have known each other. I thought I was finally rid of you when your father cast you out, but you are so relentless that you rallied the gremlins to accomplish something no other exile had ever achieved and for all of that, you come for me. I don't want you, I never wanted you and I never will want you, you arrogant, pompous ass! For anyone else, I would consider mercy, but you have long since exhausted that option. If you would bring war upon our peaceful city for your selfish desires, then I would send you to the deepest dungeon and lock every door between your cell and the surface!"

Zeke was even more shocked. "I honestly had no idea you had such venom and vitriol within you. If it weren't directed at me, I'd find such passion even more attractive."

Kyra clenched her fists. “Never have I so regretted that I have neither the blades of a fencer nor the surplus voltage for electrokinesis and must rely on the most mundane of means to mete out justice upon you.”

Just then the front door burst open and imperial soldiers entered the bureau. Gol was startled long enough for Zeke to move out of reach from his captor and ran to his soldiers. “Retreat!” Zeke disappeared among his soldiers and they backed out.

Gol and Kat stepped forward to pursue Zeke, but Kyra raised her hand to stop them. “Don’t bother, let him go.”

“Are you sure?” Kat asked.

Kyra nodded. “Pursuing him will most likely lead to a trap, do not give him that advantage. He will need time to heal his wound, until then we can better plan our next move. We won this round today, let us be satisfied with that.” Kyra tried to sound confident and resolute, but her friends could see her shaking, barely able to stand.

Kat held her friend to keep her from falling. “Are you okay?”

“Yes.” Kyra nodded. “Yes, I am fine now. Can you escort me to the chambers of the High Council? I am sure we are going to have to discuss today’s events and determine what we will have to do next in response.”

“Are you sure that is our highest priority right now?” Gol asked. “Are you sure you don’t want some time to recover?”

Kyra shook her head. “No, the others need to know about Zeke. I won’t be able to rest until I know that matter is being properly attended to.” With Gol and Kat at her side, Kyra made her way to the central chamber of the Bureau to meet with the other Engineers.

Chapter 11

It was hard to hear anything over the muttering of the engineers gathered in the chamber of the high council. There had not been any comparable conflict in living memory, even the eldest had no stories to share of anything like this. The most common violent act was releasing such energy in fencing matches, otherwise there were only rare occasional assaults which were usually put on trial and resulted in exile. So many engineers were talking about the day's events nobody could hear what was being said.

Cidolfas entered the chamber and took the center as the head of the council and slammed a gavel to get everyone's attention. "Order, order! We are all distressed over what has just occurred. It is entirely unprecedented. However, we must stand united to preserve our society, and that starts with an ordered discussion. It would seem that the exiles have united and came back for revenge. The question is, how were they able to secure resources to become such a formidable force?"

"It was Zeke." Kyra called out.

The council gasped together loudly. Cidolfas addressed Kyra. "How do you know this?"

"He came for me." Kyra replied. "My friends here were able to protect me and force him into retreat, but he made it clear he was their leader. He called himself Emperor and wanted me to be his Empress. The only reason they retreated was because one of my companions wounded him."

Cidolfas furrowed his brow in concern but did not deny the claim. "It seems I may have been too merciful in merely exiling my son and too shortsighted in his potential. They have retreated for the time being, but it seems there are forces making camp on the border. It can only be assumed they are waiting for their Emperor to lead them into action again and that we only have until there has been suitable recovery in their ranks and leadership and they will make another strike. We have survived this far by pure luck. Hunters and Fencers will not be enough to fight off an army like this when they strike next, we must prepare our own standing military."

"Are we going to fit all of these new soldiers with cyberblades?" One Engineer asked.

Cidolfas shook his head. "No, the process of integrating weaponry into civilians has always been a tricky proposition that our current system limits properly. When this is over, we don't need an unnecessary swelling of combat ready cyborgs burdened with weapons meant for what will hopefully be a short-term war. However, we will need to make sure there is an organized front to handle the sheer numbers. We will contact the Hunter's Guild to organize volunteers, the Smiths will prepare armor and weapons. Those with any experience before today will be organized as officers according to skill to lead the new recruits and maintain the guard at the edge of the city. Anyone unable to contribute to the military effort will be moved to the far side of the city for safety. It would also help if we could get some intelligence regarding the invading forces, and this may be the hardest part. I can't imagine there is anyone in our society that is particularly suited for espionage, but if anyone does know of anyone who could help in that area, please enlist their help. I know, such individuals may be getting their experiences from illegal activity but for the greater good, they shall be forgiven any transgressions if they can help us get through these trying times. Gol, please let the Smiths know about the order for standard weaponry. Kat, there were many casualties, and while I thank you for helping Kyra, I believe you are needed with the other Healers. Kyra, I will trust you with reaching out to the Hunter's Guild. You are dismissed to your duties."

The three youths left the room as ordered, trusting their elders to make tactical preparations for war. Gol looked to his companions, thinking about how long he had known them and how much it would have hurt to lose either one today or even if he lost them in the days to come. First, he turned to Kyra. "Are you sure you're going to be okay? Today was a lot and you haven't had any combat experience like Kat and I have."

Kyra nodded. "We grew up on a farm together and that was tough enough, though this office may have softened me up a bit. Perhaps I needed some action to light a fire under me. I trust I will be fine among the Hunters." With that she walked off.

Gol then turned to Kat and hugged her close. "Hinu help me if anything had happened to you." He then kissed her as if it may be the last time as he feared it could possibly be.

Kat held Gol for a long moment sharing his feelings. When she finally pulled away, she released her cyber blade and looked at the blood from when she wounded Zeke. For the first time since it happened, she allowed herself to feel what she had done. She began to cry. "What have I done Gol? I am a Healer, I'm not supposed to cause harm like this. My cyberblade was for fencing and emergency defense."

"And that's what it was, emergency defense." Gol reassured her. "You had to protect Kyra. You are still a defender and a healer. The fact that you feel so upset proves your heart is in the right place and I am proud of you for taking action when necessary."

"Thank you." Kat replied through tears. Before she could say anything else, she had caught another glimpse of her bloody blade and turned to vomit in a potted plant. "I'm sorry."

"No, don't be." Gol reassured her again. "I don't know if I would have handled it much better if I had been the one to maim Zeke. It should have been me, you don't deserve this burden."

"No one does." Kat said. "We live in such a perfect world, or at least it seemed that way until Zeke ruined everything. How could things have gone so wrong?"

"Envy is an ugly thing." Gol replied. "He was sure he was meant to rule, and he is not going to stop until he gets his way."

"Are we going to have to kill him?" Kat asked.

Gol paused in thought. "I hope it doesn't come to that. But I had hoped it wouldn't go this far." They embraced again before going their separate ways, still holding hands until the last moment.

Gol went to the Forge as ordered, and along the way he could see the damage that had been done to the city along the way. He could tell exactly which direction the invasion had come from as the damage got worse as he got closer to the source at the edge of the city. Smoke rose from some buildings still smoldering from fire damage. There were already many trying to repair the damage, but they were clearly outnumbered compared to their workload. The rebuilding effort was going to be a long road and most likely Gol and his fellow Smiths were going to be busy for the foreseeable future.

Gol made it to the Forge and found that it was largely undamaged and most of his fellows were already hard at work. "Good to see at least one place seems to be still standing strong."

Angus greeted his apprentice with arms wide open. "We Smiths are too strong to be taken down by gremlins! But I shouldn't have to tell you that my friend and proud warrior! I take it my best Fencer held his own on the battlefield, eh?"

"And then some!" Gol replied. "But the Empire is not done with us yet. They will strike again, and we need to arm our people for the next wave. I've got an order from the Bureau of Engineers to make as many weapons and armor as we possibly can."

Angus nodded. "Sounds like it's time for my emergency war ration plan."

Gol raised an eyebrow. "What's that?"

"Exactly what it sounds like." Angus said. "We have made swords for fencing and arrow heads for the Hunters and even armor, but much of it has been low priority due to low need. But I always had a plan to redirect resources just in case we ever needed it. We haven't needed it so far, so it's stayed just an idea, but the time has come."

Go, hung his head. "I hoped this day would never come."

Angus put his hand on Gol's shoulder. "We all feel that way. But wishing it didn't happen will not make it so. Only doing our part will make things right. Now get to work, you're good with swords and gauntlets so make as many as you can, alternate back and forth, finish one, start the other, don't stop until last light. I'll go around and let everyone else know what they need to do."

Gol collected his materials and went to his workstation. As his hammer rang out against his anvil, Gol began to feel at ease for the first time since the invasion began. Working on a project that was constructive towards the effort to defend the city was just what he needed. As he got to work, he noticed a movement in the shadow of his workshop. After a moment, a familiar figure came forth from the shadows. "Kewpie? What are you doing here?" His mole-bat waddled over to his scrap pile and brought a piece of metal over to him. "Are you my assistant now? Well, I appreciate it, but you'd better be ready, we have a lot to do." The mole-bat squealed back seemingly in delight.

* * *

Kat walked through the wreckage of the city that Gol had merely looked upon. She needed to reach the wounded at the edge where most of the violence had taken place. The Healers had already gathered around the wounded and started trying to treat everyone they could. The entire guild had gathered already searching for any survivors. Their faces were stained with tears over those who were already too far gone. Never had they seen so much injury and blood. There was sickness, and the occasional accidental injury from everyday activities and fencers needed to be cared for after matches, but the sheer volume of these violent injuries was entirely unprecedented. The known history of the Technocracy had no records of anything like this, not one, not all of it combined. The Healers were not ready for this, but they were trying their best. They had even resorted to using carbuncles and mandragoras for extra hands because the wounded far outnumbered the Healers, even with these makeshift assistants there were still too many patients to care for. Kat's carbuncle was even among those already hard at work and greeted her as soon as she arrived.

Wandering through the camp, Kat finally reached Ruby. When Ruby looked up at her apprentice, she smiled a strained smile through tears as she ran to embrace her. "Oh my child, I am so grateful you are unharmed. All this time I feared you may be the next body brought to me. I am also grateful you are here to help, at least I hope you are. We need all the help we can get." Ruby let out a huge sigh, unable to think of what else to say, only gesturing at those in need. "I don't even know where to begin. How did this even happen?"

"It was Zeke." Kat said.

Ruby was shocked. "The son of Cidolfas? Wasn't he exiled for nearly killing his opponent in the fencing arena?"

Kat nodded. "He gathered his fellow exiles and built an empire with his own army. They are armed with weapons called guns that can fire projectiles and gunblades that combine that technology with swords to make the most destructive weapons we can imagine."

Ruby was not sure how to respond. "But why? Why would he do this? What could be worth this?"

Kat shook her head. "Gol says it's envy. He believes he is destined to rule and if the Technocracy will not be given over to him freely, he will take it by force."

"But there will be nothing left to conquer if he continues like this!" Ruby exclaimed. She looked to the horizon and saw that there were still troops marching just beyond the edge of the city, right now specks in the distance, but they could return at any moment. Her lips trembled and she collapsed, overwhelmed by the thought that this might only be the beginning.

"Cidolfas has a plan, we will rise up against this threat!" Kat tried to encourage her mentor.

"Rise up?" Ruby said. "Do you mean we will fight? More fighting means more wounded. How much more can we take?"

"All of it." Kat replied with confidence that even surprised her. "We are Healers, this is what we do! For now, we will heal these wounded, prepare the strong for the fight, move the weak to safety, but we will not give up on our duty to save every life we can!"

"We have already failed so many though." Ruby replied crestfallen.

"But those who yet live still need us and we will not let them down!" Kat said resolute. She wasn't sure where her positive energy was coming from, this had been by far the hardest day of her life, and she was exhausted physically, spiritually, and emotionally. But seeing what was happening around her she felt she had to do her part to restore order.

Kat went to get her first patient. She found one of the first victims from the raid. He had been hit by bullets but luckily only a few and they hadn't hit any vital organs. How this happened beyond sheer luck nobody could say, but ultimately, he had only suffered blood loss and needed rest and plenty of fluids. First, the bullets had to be removed, and most of them had been, but the surgeon was tiring. "I can take over." Kat offered, she had less experience, but at this point the tired surgeon who had clearly been working on other patients was not much better and with a weary and handed his tools over to her. After she pulled the last bullet and bandaged her patient, Kat brought him a potion that helped rehydrate him as well as restore protein and iron levels. Using focused electrokinesis, she was able to direct the flow within his body to optimize healing rates. His recovery would still be long, but not as long as it would have been without care.

As she tried to focus her energy on helping her patient heal, she glanced to the side and saw that not everyone was as lucky as her patient. On either side, they had resorted to phoenix down, on one side the patient gasped back to life coming back from the brink, the other however was too far gone even for the miraculous restorative properties of the feathers. The Healers covered the face of the deceased with a blanket and moved them to the side to make room for the next patient. The dead were beginning to pile up, they didn't even have a place to put them yet and no time for it when other lives had to be saved. Kat cried but had time for few tears before she had to wipe them away and move on to the next patient. Some were bullet wounds requiring surgery, others were burns requiring aloe balm, still others had broken bones from falling as they ran or being crushed under debris, but there were so many it was hard to tell which was which anymore, the Healers barely had time to determine treatment and provide it before blurring straight into the next one.

"Next." Kat called for her next patient, going through the motions as a living machine at this point.

"There is no next patent." Ruby replied. "We finally provided care to all who need it, at least all that we could save. Now they must rest, and so must we." Ruby directed Kat to a couple of empty cots. "We don't have the time or energy to go home, let us just rest here."

Kat barely touched the mat before she passed out, too tired to even dream.

* * *

Meanwhile Kyra had her own challenge. She made her first visit to the Hunter's Guild headquarters. She had never been to the Dragon's Bane tavern before, she never needed to, but there was a first time for everything. When she arrived, it seemed to be empty. "Hello? Is anybody here?"

A woman who appeared to be younger than Kyra came out from behind the bar. "Nope, just me, Jessie the receptionist, to let anyone coming by know the guild is closed until further notice."

"Why is the guild closed?" Kyra asked. "We need the guild more than ever with the siege going on!"

Jessie laughed. "Well, that's exactly why the guild is closed! Every Hunter has been redirected to the front lines, all other contracts are on hold. Unless you're looking to enlist, you might as well leave."

"Actually, I was here to recruit the guild on behalf of the Engineers of the Technocracy." Kyra replied. "I guess I may be late."

"We don't need to be recruited to protect our city." Jessie replied. "We may often be the most greedy, selfish, ruthless band of rascals in the city, but this is our home and we'll be damned if anybody worse is just going to take the streets from us without a fight. Having said that, if you have a contract to offer to fund and support our efforts, we're not too proud to accept. Would you like me to direct you to the camp?"

"Well, yes." Kyra was surprised at how well this was turning out. She had expected this was going to be harder. Now she could only assume her friends had much harder tasks on hand considering they had actual work they could not avoid. Most of her challenge had already been mitigated before she even arrived.

"I can't leave." Jessie clarified as she pulled out a map. "I have to deal with the other stragglers, but I can tell you where to go and join the others. The reports suggest that they came from the North, and we determined that there was little from East or West, so we narrowed down the point of entry here." She pointed to a part of the map at most Northern part of the city. "That's where we set up camp. The Healers set up camp just South of the Hunters' camp so the Hunters can protect those who can't be moved, and the Healers can be ready for the first to be wounded from battle once the next wave begins."

"Thank you." Kyra said. "One more thing, do you know anything about any other fencers? We could use every fighter we can get."

"Again, we're way ahead of you." Jessie replied. "Most of the fencers have already enlisted with the Hunters and those that haven't are either working on repairs from this battle or preparing supplies for the next. But every fencer that registered for cyberblades has been accounted for and promised they will come to call once the fighting starts. Is there anything else I can help you with?"

"No, I think that's all." Kyra replied with a slight respectful bow. "Thank you, I'd best be off to the Hunters' camp now." With that, Kyra left the tavern and began her journey across the city.

For the most part Kyra felt like a salmon swimming upstream, everybody else she came across was moving away from the side of the city she was traveling towards. The more north she went, the clearer the devastation had been. As she reached the very edge of the city, she came across the Healers' camp. She was tempted to visit with her friend, but when she noticed how busy they were, she changed her mind, realizing she would only get in the way of life saving efforts, and continued.

As the Healers faded out of sight behind her, she saw the Hunters' camp. It was definitely a different set up from the Healers' camp. While the Healers had set up beds and medical supplies to tend to the wounded, all the Hunters had was weapons and other battle supplies. The Healers camp had an aura of hope, but the Hunters had an aura of wrath. This was the home of warriors and killers. The fencers sharpened their blades, not only the cyberblades, but also swords and knives, and some were sparring. Other Hunters were focusing on their archery skills, which was less celebrated as sport or martial art, but for Hunters who found themselves lacking in electrokinesis, the ability to take down their quarry at a distance using a more mundane method was important. After the invasion, they couldn't afford to ignore any combat skills, so while the archers were usually the lowest of all Hunters, anyone who could land a shot was valued and being prepared to support the vanguard. If any Hunter had an ego, they were setting it aside for fear of the Empire.

Just beyond the edge of the camp and the Technocracy's capital city, the Imperial Camp could be seen. From a distance it looked quite similar, but with much more metal. Smoke filled the air blocking the sky and reeking of toxic chemicals. Bright lights illuminated the camp using a technology the Technocracy had forbidden, a light that seemed calming and yet at the same time far too strong. Soldiers marched on the horizon waiting the orders from their superiors that they had regrouped and were ready to strike again. The enemy stayed behind an invisible line and the tension could be felt by everyone in the Technocratic militia.

Kyra could not believe what she was seeing in the enemy camp, there were machines she was sure the Technocracy would not allow and exceeded any expectations of what she thought could exist. Some other machines looked like metal giant people. She had no idea what powered them, or how they could be operated in any way. “What even are those things?” She thought out loud.

“War mechs.” The answer came from a large man who Kyra presumed was the leader of the Hunters. “That’s what we’ve heard them called by the imperial soldiers. They are controlled by a single soldier each from the inside. They are slow but those who have witnessed what they are capable of and lived to tell the tale have said they are formidable weapons. They have guns that are larger and more powerful than the weapons foot soldiers carry. The feet along can crush an entire person.”

“Wow.” Kyra replied, quickly realizing they had not been properly introduced. “I’m sorry, I’m Kyra, I’m an Engineer, I was sent by the High Council. May I ask your name?”

“My name’s Mack, and I’m the leader of the Hunter’s Guild. May I ask what brings one of our highest officials down here to such a dangerous location?”

“I’m not that high actually.” Kyra said rather flustered. “I was raised on a farm and got lucky on my exams to move up in the world. But the High Council is concerned about the threat to our city and people, and I was sent to hire and organize your guild, but it looks like you have things under control already.”

Mack laughed. “I guess you could say your work here is done. But before we send you on your way, there is a way you could help us. We managed to take down a war mech, but it was a very difficult challenge and if you could analyze the wreckage and help us determine a more effective means of destroying them, we would appreciate it. We know how to hunt ordinary living creatures, but when it comes to machines, all the best and brightest were picked up by your people."

Kyra perked up a little. "Of course I can help! I was feeling a bit disappointed that I came all this way for nothing, but if I can help I gladly will. So where is this wreckage?"

"Right this way." Mack waved to Kyra and started walking to the other side of the camp farther from the enemy lines. "We needed to keep the war mech as far away from the enemy as possible because we don't want them knowing what we've got. As far as we know, they don't even know they lost a unit." Mack directed Kyra inside a tent facing away from the enemy. Inside the tent was what was left of a war mech, though it was definitely in a state where it was best described in past tense. The arms and legs had all been separated from the torso, every part had at least two holes, and wires and gears were protruding from every opening. "Sorry about how torn up it is, but we couldn't collect it without fully incapacitating it."

"Dare I ask what happened to the operator?" Kyra queried.

Mack shook his head. "He refused to go quietly. When we stopped the mech he engaged in hand-to-hand combat and refused to give up until...well, you know, the inevitable end of a fight with a relentless foe. The mech is in better shape than he was."

Kyra started looking over the left arm, the most familiar part. She tried looking through the holes at the parts inside. "It looks a lot like a regular cyberarm, only on a larger scale. I would imagine they mostly used the basics of cybernetics and extrapolated from there. I'll check the legs if I can find any particular unique weaknesses we can take advantage of, but it's probably going to be just unique flaws in basic design. What I really need to examine is the central body, the controls and most importantly the power source. I'm very curious about the power source, normally we rely on bioelectricity, but there's no way anyone could produce enough energy to operate something this large on bioelectricity alone. Most cyborgs only produce enough to operate one arm, some have more power but even the strongest would be exhausted just trying to walk on these legs a short distance. They must have come up with some sort of artificial energy source. Of course, if I could figure out what that source is and how to cut it off, that would help the Hunters disable the mechs much more efficiently."

"Sounds like you have your work cut out for you." Mack said just a little too cheerfully. "If you need any assistance, let me know, otherwise I have to oversee training and keep an eye on the enemy. Good luck, and I really mean that, if you can figure out an easier way to take these things down it may mean all the difference when the fighting starts."

"I'll do my best sir." Kyra bid farewell to Mack while already dismantling the torso and trying to analyze its inner workings. "Let's see what makes you tick." There was no head to the robot, where the head should have been was the pilot seat and the rest was large enough to fit around that. From the seat, Kyra started prying apart any loose panel she could find to get a closer look underneath. Then she found something familiar that scared her when she first saw it and realized she knew exactly what it was. "A combustion engine. Wain must have joined the Empire. That would explain a lot. Four cylinders, one for each limb. The primary controls seem to direct fuel where it needs to be controlled the most, walk mode alternates the lower half in sync automatically, the upper half relies on some more complicated controls for more precise movement. It'll take time to understand exactly how the arms work, but this seems like a solid start, I definitely figured out the heart of this damn thing. And I'm talking to myself, genius with nobody to hear it, tragedy." She examined a little closer and figured out where the fuel tank was, or rather had been. It had been damaged during the fight, which she realized was how the Hunters had stopped it in the first place, a lucky shot had ignited the fuel tank and caused an explosion. The Hunters probably didn't realize what they had done, but now that she knew what worked, they could start work on a strategy that targeted this weakness.

After tinkering around for hours, Kyra went to check in with Mack. "I figured out how it works, the main thing is the engine, which is on the back, which relies on a fuel tank right next to it. The fuel is highly flammable so if you can hit the tank with anything flammable that's how to break it down, and I think that's what you did with the first one. But that's definitely the spot if you want to get it over quick."

Mack smiled. "That's great news! I don't suppose you know enough to get that one running so we can use it against them?"

Kyra grimaced. "Yes and no. Depending on how much help I can get it can be put back together and functions restored. However, the problem is that fuel source is hard to obtain. I happen to know it's more trouble than it's worth, so no, we can't get it running again."

Mack stroked his chin. "Is the fuel really that hard to get? I wonder how they are able to work with it."

"For starters, all the smoke and that smell that goes with it is part of it." Kyra began to explain. "They're burning petroleum, it's hard to get and while it gets the job done it's toxic. If they're using it at home, it's probably even worse than what we are witnessing here."

Mack's eyes went wide. "Is it really that bad? Well, the bigger they are the harder they fall. They are strong but slow, if we know how to take them down quick, that may give us enough of an advantage, we just break the damn things before they can get to us. Let's see how tough they are when we take away their toys!"

"Is there anything else I can do to help?" Kyra asked.

Mack rested his hand on her shoulder. "I appreciate your enthusiasm, but you've done quite enough today. It's getting late, go ahead and go home, report back to the High Council, and if there's anything the higher ups think is worth sending you back for, we'll see you then."

Before Kyra could argue, she yawned and conceded she was tired. "It has been a long day. Good night." Kyra used the last of her energy for the day just to get home and as soon as she got home, she collapsed on her bed and knew nothing until the sunrise through her window woke her up.

* * *

The next morning was somber, after all efforts to save those that could be saved, those that could not were given a mass funeral. There had never been a mass funeral in living memory, usually only person died at a time, it was rare to even get as many as a dozen at once, and almost always of natural causes. This attack on their peaceful civilization had left a mark that would not soon be forgotten. All the families of those that were lost gathered at the graveyard while those who didn't lose loved ones, especially the Hunters, tried to keep the city running. The Healers were called for ceremonial purposes, and Kat invited Kyra and Gol for moral support.

The three friends gathered to observe the procession. One by one, the caskets were carried into the graveyard. Each one was carried by the family of the fallen, each one barely holding it together. Dozens came in, a whole new section had to be added to the graveyard for those that died during this tragedy, but it wasn't until hundreds gathered around their fallen to see them off for the last time that anyone fully realized the magnitude of the event. Each family remained circled around their dead, the crowd extending as far as the eye could see, and the farthest away could barely see the community leaders. The caskets were set down next to the holes dug for their graves, each one with a tombstone with a hole for the cyberarm. Part of the funeral ceremony involved placing the cyberarm in the custom-made slot where it would be part of the memorial to be seen by everyone.

Now was time for the Healers to take on their most difficult task, healing not the body but the soul. Healers were responsible for the lives of their people right up until the end and then one last time, to see them off and heal their families from the loss. It was not an easy task at all, at least when healing the living there was always hope that success meant the patient would walk away proudly, but a funeral was acknowledging the inevitable defeat of mortality that all would have to face. Usually only one had to be faced at a time, but to see half the city gathered knowing each person had experienced a loss and that hundreds had reached the end of their journeys through life at once felt like a massive failure on the part of the guild. They knew it wasn't that simple, but the sheer numbers made it hard to not feel the weight of the loss. But still, they had to instill hope in those that remained to carry on.

Ruby stepped forward. "Children of Hinu, the god of electricity gives us all two gifts, the gift of life and the gift of cybernetics. Neither of these gifts are ours to keep forever, eventually comes the time they must be returned. The spark of life is put into our soul, and it grows and extends into our cybernetics, then peaks and then wanes slowly until the day it becomes no more than the spark it was when it began, to return to the father where it came from. Usually this takes years, and one lives a full life, but sometimes, the length of a blessed life is cut short. It has been a great, unprecedented tragedy that has returned so many sparks to Hinu at once, with so many of them seeming to still have so much lie left to live, children who did not even receive their arms, parents who shall not see their children grow. The sacred order of Healers tried to save as many as we could, but alas, it seems Hinu has called these souls home and it falls upon us to see them off, mourn the loss and carry on without them. Join me now in the Song of Farewell."

In the night, there is naught but dark,
But in the morn, comes the light of one spark.
Flickers in, the dawn of day,
Brighter grows, the longer stay.
The zenith reached, complete by noon,
Shine still longer, night come none too soon.
But try we might, to keep the spark,
Night will fall and bring the dark.
And though we miss, that bright warm glow,
Our time must come, this we know.

The spark leaves the metal hand,

The body returns to the land.
Broken apart, what once was whole,
We now say farewell to your soul.

Chapter 12

There was little time to rest or mourn, the next day everyone was back to work. Gol had a load of weapons and armor to deliver to the front lines, so he loaded up a cart and attached his silverwing to carry as much as possible. Kat noticed him passing by the Healers' Camp with his silverwing and Kewpie and joined him. "Hey Gol, what have you got there?"

"Swords, armor and arrow heads for the Hunters." Gol replied. "How are your patients doing?"

"Well enough." Kat replied glancing back over her shoulder. "It was touch and go for a while, but everybody is stable now, no fear that anyone will be dying soon. A t least not anymore. Anyway, I could use a change of scenery, and I'd like to see Kyra again."

"She's up there?" Gol asked.

"Yeah, didn't she tell you?" Kat asked. "She went up to organize the Hunters on behalf of the Engineers. They didn't need her for that, but they wanted her to analyze enemy technology, and she's been up there ever since."

"And you thought she might be at a stage where she might need a hand or two?" Gol asked.

Kat rolled her eyes with mock innocence. "Maybe."

"I guess you can help me unload the goods when we get there." Gol conceded. Once they reached their destination, they took turns grabbing loads off the cart and setting them down where they belonged. As they finished dropping off their delivery, they were greeted almost immediately by Kyra. "Gol, Kat! It's great to see you again!"

"Yes, great to see you too, but we did just see each other yesterday at the funeral." Gol pointed out. "Is there perhaps another reason why you might be happy to see us?"

"No fooling you is there?" Kyra replied. "I have been working on a plan to disable the enemy war mechs before they can be used in the next attack, and I need help carrying out that plan."

"We get to play spies and saboteurs?" Kat asked with way too much enthusiasm for Gol's liking.

"You shouldn't sound so excited." Gol corrected her. "This sounds like a very dangerous mission."

Kat pouted. "We haven't had a quality adventure since the quest for the phoenix down! Let's do this!"

"It is dangerous." Kyra confirmed. "But it will be even more dangerous to not do anything. Come with me." She directed them to join her in her work tent and showed them the remnants of the war mech she had been working on. "Behold!"

"What is that?" Gol asked.

"A war mech." Kyra answered. "Or at least it was. Unfortunately, there's more where that came from. Fortunately, studying this one I have figured out how to break down others even more easily than this one went down. The problem is that it involves explosions which are dangerous and, more importantly from a tactical standpoint, loud. Once we start blowing up machines, we'll draw attention, so it's kind of a one-shot deal to coordinate as much destruction as possible before they come for us. And that means we need as many people on this as possible."

"I suppose if it's for the greater good." Gol said resigned.

"Okay, you'll need these." Kyra collected some explosives and handed them to her friends. "Be very careful, it doesn't take much for these to explode. But what we're looking for is to make the explosion big enough to blow apart the metal, and to do that you need to hit the fuel tank here." Kyra pointed to the back of the mech. "The fuel is highly flammable so if you set the explosive here, then the fuel will magnify the explosion. This whole thing relies on the fuel source, so long as we take out the fuel, whatever is left is just a hunk of useless metal. Of course, they could probably replace the fuel tank, so the more damage you do, the harder it will be to repair. Aim for maximum destruction!"

Gol was shocked at the smiles on the faces of his friends. "What happened to the sweet girls I grew up with on the farm?"

"Our home got attacked." Kat replied. "They woke the beast in us."

"Is there anything else we need to know about this plan?" Gol asked.

"We'll strike at dusk." Kyra said. "Until then, check in with the other hunters and coordinate with them to see if there is anything else they've figured out that you need to know."

"You mean you didn't think of everything yourself?" Gol asked.

Kyra shrugged. "I figured out the basic mechanics of the machines, the guild regulars handle personnel logistics. Now, go on, shoo!" Kyra waved them off and went back to tinkering with the mech.

Gol noticed Kyra tinkering. "I don't suppose there's any chance you can figure out how to use these weapons for our side?"

Kyra shook her head vigorously. "Absolutely not. The fuel is petroleum oil, it's difficult to obtain and even worse to use."

"Petroleum oil?" Gol noted. "I remember learning about that in school. Usually, it's found in shale deposits in mines, and sometimes larger purer deposits in other underground wells. But there's no way to remove it without contaminating the ground, and burning it contaminates the air, which is why the technocracy banned it. No wonder it smells so bad over there. I wonder how much damage they did to their own land to get their supply. Do you think that's why they came here? They damaged their own land so much they needed fresh land to work with."

"Possibly." Kyra agreed. "All the more reason to stop them before they get here."

"Come on Gol!" Kat called. "We need to meet with the other scouts! We haven't got all day here! Let's go!"

"Coming dear!" Gol called back.

Gol and Kat went to rendezvous with the other Hunters. There wasn't much to talk about once they laid out their plans for who was placing their bombs and where, they just brushed up on their combat skills in case things got violent. They spent the rest of the day sparring and watching the sun drop in the sky.

The sky turned orange as the sun set. Gol and Kat met up on the western hill to get a good view of the sun's last light, half obscured by clouds of smog from the North. Kat leaned up against Gol. "Brings back memories."

"Of what exactly?" Gol asked Kat.

"The quest for the phoenix down of course!" Kat replied. "I think I can almost see the burning mountains from here."

"Really?" Gol asked, trying to see the mountains too.

Kat laughed. "No, it's too far away to see. You are so gullible it's cute." She gave him a kiss on the cheek. They sat quietly watching the sun set slowly, feeling every second knowing what would happen when the last rays of light faded over the horizon, both dreading it and anticipating it in equal measure. They silently counted down the very last seconds, and then it was dark.

Almost immediately their silent vigil was interrupted by a messenger calling them to duty. "It's time guys, let's go!"

Everybody grabbed their explosives and started moving into the camp. Stealth was key, moving in shadows, making as little noise as possible. Everybody moved to a war mech, and if it was claimed they went to another one, going farther into the camp until every Hunter was positioned at a different machine. Kat and Gol were the last to get into position, which meant they were the deepest into the camp and would get things started signaling everyone else. They looked at each other, set the explosives in place on the fuel tanks, moved a safe distance away, and then both shot an electric bolt at the fuses. It only took a few seconds for the fuses to burn and the bombs to detonate. The blast was intensive enough to knock the machines over, landing on their front sides. Gol and Kat started running before the war mechs hit the ground. As they ran, the other Hunters detonated their explosives in response to the signal and joined them in their retreat. As the mob of retreating hunters grew larger, so did the trail of destruction they left in their wake, and none of the imperials knew whether to focus on the Hunters or the damage that was being done. The Hunters took advantage of the confusion to escape. Some of the soldiers took focus on the Hunters and attacked, but the Hunters were prepared and came back with their own counter attacks.

Just as Gol and Kat were running out of breath, they saw the line between camps and crossed the line to safety. They looked back and saw that most of the others were following right behind and the those that weren't keeping up were just held back by the soldiers, but they were holding their own in the fight.

As soon as they caught their breath, Gol and Kat hurried to Kyra to report the successful mission. Unfortunately, when they reached her, they found they were not the only ones who had crossed enemy lines. Zeke was there, now with two arms, and both with blades extended in a most threatening manner toward Kyra. "A reunion so soon. Did you all miss me that much?"

"How did you get a new arm so fast?" Gol asked.

"That's your first question?" Zeke replied with disappointment. "You should know I wouldn't come unprepared. Having just one arm is so old fashioned. I got an extension cord to draw power from my left side to operate my right side. It only took a couple days to make the necessary adjustments. Do you want to see a demonstration of my new improved abilities?" Without waiting for a response, he turned to fight Gol and Kat, striking both at once.

Gol and Kat were ready for Zeke and both countered. Despite Zeke's best efforts, they remained in synch matching him blow for blow while never getting in each other's way. The fight seemed to continue without end, random cycles of the same moves without anyone giving up a moment of weakness. Gol even grabbed a spare sword to double up on Zeke but even the extra blade didn't seem to be making much of a difference in slowing Zeke down. But then Gol and Kat pulled off an unexpected finishing move, recoiling from a strike high overhead and spinning low faster than Zeke could follow. They cut through both his legs and brought him down literally and figuratively. They crossed their blades across Zeke's throat. "Give it up Zeke, it's over." Gol said.

Zeke just laughed maniacally. "You still don't understand, I will never give up as long as I live. Finish what you started if you have the guts or accept defeat from me!"

"What are you talking about?" Gol asked. "Are you delusional? We just cut off your legs and now we have our blades at your throat about to kill you. How do you think you still have a chance to win here? You literally don't have a leg to stand on."

Zeke snapped his fingers and a robot barged in knocking Gol and Kat out of the way and picking up Zeke in a single fluid movement. "You continue to underestimate me! I always have a back-up plan! I will admit, this set back will take some time to recover from, but I will not be leaving empty-handed!" The robot released tentacles that grabbed Kyra and pulled her close holding her prisoner against the machine's body. The robot then ran off with its passengers and Gol and Kat gave chase.

As the robot sped up, Gol and Kat whistled for their silverwings which came running with Kewpie and Kat's carbuncle holding on for dear life. Gol and Kat mounted the birds as they ran by and didn't break pace for a moment. They continued to race after the robot with more speed, but as they got closer the robot transformed, dropping to the ground on wheels that seemed to form out of its legs and arms. In the new configuration, Kyra was still bound behind Zeke who was steering the new vehicle and picked up pace to outrun the bird riders. Still, they refused to give up and kept running after him, looking for a chance to catch up and reclaim Kyra.

As Zeke tried to escape the Hunters' camp, some of the Hunters tried to attack him, recognizing that he must be the enemy because they did not recognize him as an ally with his unfamiliar vehicle. Unfortunately, the wits to recognize him didn't mean they had the wits to win a fight with him. He was able to cut down every hunter that he was foolhardy enough to try, and he had no guilt about the blood trail he left behind. Eventually he crossed the line between the two camps, Gol and Kat did not give up, but once they crossed into enemy lines, they were alone, as all other Hunters had retreated to their own camp and were trying to hold the line against retaliation.

The change in the tone of the chase could be felt immediately, now everyone was attacking Gol and Kat trying to protect Zeke from them. However, the silverwings were faster and nimbler than the imperials expected, dodging and weaving between the troops. Kat and her carbuncle amplified a protective forcefield to reduce the risk of injury, while Gol did his best to fight off whoever got through their defenses. Gol was focused enough to fight any enemy that came after him or Kat without letting even one slow them down. The cyborgs, their steeds and their carbuncle were working together as one unified team, Kewpie was the only one not contributing anything other than squeals of fear.

Zeke wasn't slowing down and he didn't need to as he knew the layout of the camp and anyone who was in his way moved for their Emperor. Anyone with the wits and reflexes turned to fight the pursuers, but many were not fast enough. Nobody had expected a mounted cavalry to race through much less prepare any kind of counterattack, they had the element of surprise on their side. Still, what they really needed now was speed and they didn't quite have enough. Eventually Zeke got to his destination, his airship on the far side of the camp. Zeke tried to board the airship but needed to slow down just enough that he lost his lead and Gol and Kat finally caught up to him. However, their victory was not completely assured, as Zeke used the momentum to throw a still bound Kyra through the door into the airship while transforming his vehicle back to a robot to engage his pursuers.

"I'll give you this, you made it farther than I thought." Zeke said. "But this ends now!" Using the extended limbs of his robot body he blocked Gol and Kat from moving any farther. The silverwings skidded to a stop before they were sliced up by Zeke's cyberblades, but Gol and Kat were undeterred and jumped off their birds and straight into the fight ready to parry with their own cyberblades. Their first strike appeared to be offensive but was actually defensive as they were using the movement to protect themselves from Zeke while still closing the distance. As they landed, they prepared for the real fight, hacking and slashing at Zeke relentlessly to keep him occupied so that he couldn't escape with Kyra in tow.

With his robot Zeke was even more agile than before, and it took everything Gol and Kyra had to keep up, the carbuncle and the birds had to do their best to distract the machine just to give them a chance. "How did you build a machine that can fight five at once?" Gol asked between blows.

"Five?" Zeke laughed. "I designed this machine to fight more than five, I'm going easy on you to conserve energy! And don't think I don't see you back there, mole-bat! I didn't lose count of how many were chasing me." Zeke turned to draw everyone's attention to Kewpie trying to break Kyra free. It was a desperate attempt to begin with but now it seemed downright futile.

Gol took advantage of the momentary distraction to strike at Zeke's back. He couldn't pierce Zeke's armor enough to hurt him, but he did cut the cable that allowed him to power his right arm. Zeke frowned as his right arm slowed down and went limp. "It seems my time having fun with you is over, I'll just leave you with our little friend here." With that he ejected himself from the robot and allowed it to take its own independent mode again with its own head back in place, still parrying every blow from Gol and Kat without missing a beat.

Zeke landed in the airship between Kyra and Kewpie. Using his good arm, he picked up the mole-bat and threw him out of the airship, the poor creature breaking his fall with his own wings. "Can I get some help here? My crippling injuries are ruining my dramatic exit!" A soldier picked him up and carried him to the helm to pilot the airship raising it into the air to fly back to the imperial capital.

Meanwhile, the battle was still going on the ground with the robot still fighting Gol and Kat and their animal companions. The robot was much faster and more agile without the extra weight of Zeke and Kyra, which made the fight much more difficult. However, this also meant that with no passengers, there was no holding back to avoid hurting a living person, so Gol started charging up his best blast. Kat and her carbuncle protected him with a force field while the silverwings and Kewpie did their best to fight or at least distract the robot until Gol finished charging his blast and released it. The blast was enough to short circuit the robot, at least for a few minutes, which was enough time for them to finish it off with straight forward physical attacks, reducing it to scrap before it could move again.

Gol and Kat looked up to see the airship disappeared in the distance beyond the dark clouds of smoke from the Empire. They looked back and saw the imperial soldiers coming for them. They quickly mounted their birds and turned to flee.

"Where are we going?" Kat asked.

"We can't make it back through the imperial siege camp, so that leaves only one direction." Gol sheathed his sword and pointed in the direction Zeke's airship was flying. "We pursue Zeke and rescue Kyra!"

Chapter 13

Kyra had been knocked unconscious when Zeke threw her in the airship and when she regained consciousness, she was on a four-poster bed in a white room. She was wearing a silk gown with a matching glove over her cyberarm and a gold tiara on her head, with no idea how she had become dressed this way or how she got here. She tried to get off the bed, finding a pair of slippers to match her gown that she slipped her feet into and looked around the room. It was the most decadent place she had ever seen, far gaudier than anything she ever saw in the Technocracy. The walls were marble with gems and gold inlaid which drew her attention for what seemed like hours.

"You're awake." Zeke's voice came from behind her. "I was wondering when you would come to. What do you think of this place?"

"It's a bit much." Kyra replied, unimpressed. Still, she kept looking around in awe despite her words.

"Your voice says no, but your eyes say yes." Zeke said. He smiled a wicked smile as he came closer to Kyra. "Nothing but the finest for my queen, my empress." He took her hand and kissed it as he tried to direct her around the room. He was wearing a silver-gray suit with a jacket with gold buttons, with matching shoes and white gloves. He looked positively regal, but still paled in comparison to Kyra.

Kyra shrugged him off. 'Where are we?"

"The Imperial palace of course." Zeke replied. "This is my home, our home."

"No, this is not my home." Kyra replied. "I want to go back to the Technocracy!"

"Perhaps one day." Zeke replied. "Soon I will claim it as part of my Empire, and then you can go wherever you like."

"No." Kyra said. "I want nothing to do with your Empire. I want to go home without you. Let me go!"

Zeke frowned. "And after I went through so much trouble to make this place just perfect for you! I think you are just hungry. I know I am after such a long journey, let us go and eat." He took her by the hand and walked her out the door of the room and proceeded to show her the rest of the palace. Every wall was equally ornate as were the embroidered rugs on the floor. He escorted her to the dining hall which was just as extravagant as every other part of the palace. The table was already set with every food Kyra had ever seen and a few she had not. Zeke pulled a chair out for her and helped her sit down. "What would you like to eat?"

Kyra looked over the food with a wary eye. "I suppose I will have a salad and some poultry with a side of steamed vegetables."

"Of course, my dear." Zeke replied, moving the items she requested closer to her so she could serve herself. "And some white wine to go with the poultry." He poured out a glass of wine for her and a glass of red wine for himself. He put together a plate with steak and herb roasted potatoes and beans for himself and sat at the table opposite from Kyra. He began to eat while his eyes remained on Kyra the whole time.

Kyra ate but had a hard time enjoying her meal. She was under a great deal of duress to begin with as a prisoner taken against her will, and Zeke watching her every move made her even more uncomfortable. The food did not taste right, but she was not sure whether it was the quality of the food or if it was the stress of her situation.

"Is the food not to your liking?" Zeke queried.

Kyra cocked her head at Zeke. "It's not the food that's the problem."

The exchange was so cold, they finished the main course in silence. Once they cleaned their plates and emptied their goblets, Zeke stood up and got some cake for dessert. "Here try this, perhaps you will enjoy this more."

Kyra took a bite and was surprised to find it was the most delicious thing she had ever eaten. She couldn't help but react with widened eyes and uttering "Mmm!"

Zeke laughed. "I'm glad I could find something you could enjoy!" Once they finished their dessert, he got up and helped Kyra out of her chair. "Come look around, let me show you paradise!" As they left the dining hall and went down the stairs, they stepped out into a courtyard that was equally beautiful to the interior of the palace. For the first time she saw the exterior of the palace, marble walls with gold trim much as the inside, but seeming much brighter as the walls reflected the sunlight. Every plant was a perfect shade of green, the flowers were equally perfect and came in every color of the rainbow and every shade in between. There were birds flying overhead and perching in the trees chirping and singing a bird symphony.

Kyra bent down to smell a flower, and then she noticed that it didn't smell right. She couldn't quite figure out why she felt it didn't smell right, but she knew something was wrong. "Why doesn't this smell right?"

Zeke suddenly looked flustered. "What do you mean?"

"The flower doesn't smell like a flower." Kyra repeated. She plucked the flower and handed it to Zeke. "Here you smell it."

Zeke took a whiff, and then stopped for a moment. Then he smiled. "The soil here is different, some plants grow differently and smell different. But once you get used to it, the smell will be just as sweet as you're familiar with. Here smell it again." Zeke handed the flower back

Kyra took the flower and smelled it again. This time the flower did smell sweeter and more like she expected a flower to smell like. But this was even weirder to her that the same flower could smell so differently. As she looked up in the sky, she noticed the birds seemed to be moving in an uncharacteristically repetitive pattern. She looked back at where she plucked the flower and after close examination, she could not find the broken stem and noticed an identical flower in its place. "What is going on here?"

"Whatever do you mean?" Zeke asked.

"You know what I mean." Kyra said with more confidence. "The food doesn't taste right, the flowers don't smell right, the birds don't fly right, the plants don't grow right, and why haven't I seen anybody else around?"

Zeke sighed. "I can explain."

Kyra got scared and ran. She kept running until she found the front door and exited the palace. Outside there was a city, the buildings closest to the palace seemed to be made from the same materials as the palace and were so tall she could barely see the top of them. As she ran through the streets the buildings were made of concrete, then bricks, getting shorter and shorter until there were two story houses the same build as the houses back in the Technocracy. But the whole city was empty, not a soul in sight. As Kyra kept running, she noticed she was not out of breath and her legs did not hurt.

When Kyra reached the outer wall of the city, Zeke was waiting for her, only now his suit was black. "Where do you think you are going?"

"I will ask you one last time, what is going on here?" Kyra asked. She looked down and saw her dress turning crimson. "Is this blood?"

"No, it's a glitch." Zeke replied. "I guess the ruse is over. This is a simulacrum, a false world, a controlled dream if you will. I have been working on this for a while, but not everything is quite done. I was hoping my programmers could finish the rest before you left the palace. There was so much more to show you inside, I was hoping this would last longer before I revealed the surprise."

"Why would you do this?" Kat asked, feeling like she wanted to cry, but no tears forming in the simulacrum. "What is the point of all this?"

"Because I can!" Zeke replied. "I want to prove what I am capable of which is anything! I have done so much but this paradise is the pinnacle of luxury. In here, anything is possible! And it is a solar powered facility, the only true infinite power supply, so this will last forever!"

"But it's not real!" Kyra cried.

"What is real?" Zeke asked. "Reality is just what we perceive. Different parts of the brain process different stimuli and put together an image of the word around us. Why worry about changing the whole world when I can just change the stimuli and therefore perception?" He caressed Kyra's cheek with his hand.

Kyra slapped Zeke's hand away. "If you feel that way, why did you bring me here? Why not just make a simulacrum of me?"

Zeke lowered his eyes. "I tried, but it's not the same."

"Exactly." Kyra said. "It's not the same, I want to go back to my reality. I want nothing to do with your world, your Empire or you. You're sick!"

Zeke paused for a moment. "As much as I would like to carry on this conversation, it has been brought to my attention that there are matters in the real world that require my attention." With a green flicker he disappeared into a cloud of ones and zeroes.

"Come back here you coward!" Kyra cried. When there was no response she pounded her fists against the wall, and then collapsed, whimpering, realizing that she was alone, hopelessly alone.

Chapter 14

It wasn't long before Gol and Kat outran the imperials, but they had no time to enjoy that relief. The landscape ahead was even worse than they had expected. The sky above was so dark with clouds they couldn't tell whether dawn had broken or if it was still night. The ground was even worse, there didn't appear to be any vegetation, at least no living vegetation. There were trees, but not a single leaf on any of them, the few that stood were dead and all but petrified. The streams and rivers were running dry and what water was left was a sickly green from contaminants Gol and Kat didn't want to think about. The air reeked with an odor unlike anything they had every smelled that made it hard to breathe. There was an eerie silence with no animals, just the water flowing and the wind blowing.

"It's even worse than we thought." Kat said while she picked up a large stick off the ground, a branch that had fallen from a nearby tree, as long as she was tall. She gave it a few swings and a spin before slamming it into the ground. "Sturdy enough to work as a staff, it may be the only thing around here that hasn't completely deteriorated. Zeke really did a number on this place."

"But how?" Gol asked. "It's only been a few years since he was exiled and came here. How could he do so much damage in so short a time?"

"Forbidden technology." Kat said. "There's a reason the Technocracy doesn't have all the machines he brought in. Because this is what it takes to make them. It can be done, but there is a price to be paid. The High Council knew this would happen and has been preventing us from developing that technology to prevent this from happening to our land."

Gol whistled. "I get that, but didn't Zeke realize he went too far? Why didn't he stop before it got this bad? Weren't there any warning signs?"

"Of course there were, he ignored the warnings." Kat replied. "This is what unchecked ambition looks like. He doesn't care about consequences, only what he can accomplish. This is why he couldn't become an engineer. It's not that he didn't know what he could do, it's that he didn't know when to stop."

Gol was speechless. There were simply no words to describe this desolate scene, to know this was the world that Zeke had chosen to live in because he wanted to make his own technology. Gol had grown up on a farm, a fertile verdant landscape that had been kept pure to provide for the people in the city which itself had been kept clean and beautiful in its own way. He had taken that balance for granted until now. What he saw was a complete wasteland that was in complete contrast with all he ever knew. He had no idea such a place could exist. "Are you sure it wasn't already like this before he got here?"

Kat shook her head sadly. "I have been out this way before with Hunters before Zeke was exiled. This used to be a forest, not at all unlike the ones closer to home. This wasn't like this before. This was all his handiwork."

As they continued to venture into the wasteland, they came a little too close to the water and tendrils emerged to grab at their feet. At first it was just one tendril, then more, enough to grab both cyborgs, and each of their animals, dragging them all into the water. Gol and Kat struck back with their weapons and as quickly as they freed themselves, they freed their pets which then scrambled away behind their masters for safety. The tendrils came back as part of a larger blob that emerged from the water. The blob was amorphous, constantly shifting and lacking any consistent details other than a pair of eyes and a wide gaping mouth large enough to swallow the entire travelling party in one gulp. It moaned, groaned, and roared all at the same time somehow. It reached out and tried to grab them with relentless hunger. Gol and Kat kept hitting it, but to no avail, the creature's soft flesh just bounced back from every attack, effectively invincible to any normal combat.

"Get back!" Gol shouted while gesturing toward his companions, putting himself between them and their assailant. He charged up his electricity and shot a heavy bolt at the blob. It howled in pain but did not stop, seeming to be enraged as much as it was hurt.

Kat shot a bolt of her own to back up Gol. "It's working, we just can't let up until it goes back in the water!" They went back and forth shooting bolts alternately relentlessly pushing the blob back in to the water. They retreated a safe distance and waited to see if it would come back out. Once they caught their breath, they took another look at the water and were content to realize that whatever it was had given up.

Then they heard a squeak behind them. A smaller blob had formed from the pieces they had cut off. The blue raindrop shaped creature was no bigger than Kewpie or the carbuncle and wouldn't have been able to harm either one. As soon as it recognized that all attention was on it, it squeaked again and bounced off behind some rocks.

"Aw poor thing." Kat said. "It looked so cute."

"It was part of a creature that tried to kill us." Gol reminded her.

"At that size I don't think it could be any kind of threat." Kat argued. "I'm gonna go check on it and make sure it's okay." She crept over to the rocks where it had disappeared. "Hey little guy. It's okay, you can come out, I'm not gonna hurt you." It cautiously peaked around the side of the rock it was hiding behind. "Aren't you a cute little slime?" She put her hand out to beckon it over. It rubbed up against her hand and cooed. She picked it up and put it on her shoulder.

"Are we on a rescue mission or are we collecting pets?" Gol asked angrily, trying to get Kat back on task.

Kat turned back to Gol frowning to match his anger. "This creature knows the terrain better than we do. If there are any threats, it's more likely to notice and when it freaks out next, we'll know if something is trying to kill us."

"So, you got us a security alarm?" Gol asked, then shrugged. "Okay, whatever you say, we need to move along if we're ever going to catch up to Zeke."

Remounting their silverwings, they proceeded through the next stretch of wasteland with their new traveling companion. There wasn't much to do or say as they went along. The land was just more of the same barren desolation. They were doing their best to stay away from the water and that seemed to keep them safe enough.

One of the few things that broke up the monotony of their surroundings were the oil derricks. The small mechanical towers dotted the landscape, but neither Gol nor Kat knew what they were. When they happened to drift near one that was active it emitted a familiar odor. Kat could barely stand the smell, covering her nose. "These must be where they get the fuel for their war mechs."

"I would guess this is also the source of a lot of the damage to the terrain." Gol surmised. "I still can't believe they would think it was worth all this. I mean, where do they even get food?"

"That's probably a large part of why they came back." Kat replied. "They're hungry."

They came across a most unwelcome change in the terrain. The ground was red with bright glowing cracks. It wasn't very far across, but it did stretch far enough in each direction that going around was not an option. The silverwings were wary about walking on this ground. Gol tried to prod his to try taking a step onto the ground, but its toe barely made contact before it recoiled and crowed in pain. "Great, now what do we do?"

Kat dismounted and took a closer look. She noticed her slime was not reacting. She took the creature and set it down where the silverwing had stepped but the slime was unfazed. "Interesting, the slime seems to be resistant to the heat. I have an idea. She then took the slime and rubbed it against the bottom of the feet of both birds. "Let's try this again."

They tried to sprint across before the coat of slime on the birds' feet wore off. They made it about halfway across before the slime started acting strange, quivering with fear. Before they could figure out what was wrong, the ground suddenly exploded. It was just one small burst that startled them more than anything, but the real problem was what came after. The explosion released what appeared to be a fireball about two or three times the size of their slime companion, but the really strange thing was that the fireball didn't just rise up and explode, it moved like around like it was alive, and worst of all it seemed to be actively hunting them. The startled birds fell over and started writhing in pain on the ground. The cyborgs were protected by their clothing and helped their birds up and quickly grabbed the smaller animals and threw them on the birds' backs and sent them running to the opposite side of the rift before they got burned any worse.

They tried to follow their animals, but the fireball chased after them and they had to fight back. They suspected their electricity wasn't going to cut it, and they feared the effect on their built-in cybernetics, so they used only their hand-held weapons. Gol held his sword with both hands, a style he had practiced but never actually used it in any practical setting. Kat hit it first with her staff, knocking it towards Gol, who sliced through it with his sword. The fireball was cut in two, but then both parts seemed to reform into whole entities.

"What is wrong with this place that everything is actively trying to kill us including things that shouldn't even be alive?" Gol screamed in frustration. "Now how are we supposed to beat these things? Everyone I cut down just becomes more!"

"Wait, look!" Kat pointed at the fireballs. "They're smaller. They may multiply each time we cut them, but they also get smaller."

"So we get an army of tiny fireballs instead of one big one?" Gol asked.

Kat nodded. "Trust me, just keep slashing!"

Gol started slicing and dicing and the fireballs continued to grow in number but shrink in size like Kat said. When they got small enough, Kat slammed the fireball into the ground and extinguished it into a spot of ash and soot. She continued swinging her staff and finishing off the tiny fireballs as quickly as Gol was cutting them down to size. Soon the fireball was completely extinguished, and they could finish the run over to the other side of the burning land. As they stopped to catch their breath, Gol looked at Kat and said, "If we come back this way, we definitely go around, not through."

Kat nodded. "Agreed."

They stopped and tended to all the burns and wounds sustained by themselves and their animal companions. Once everyone seemed to be in shape to move again, they remounted and continued their journey. Over the horizon they saw the city and breathed a sigh of relief that they were almost to their destination. But there was one last obstacle before they entered the city, a pack of pitbulls that were either feral or guards, but either way, they were in the way and hungry enough to be in a threatening mood.

"We don't have to kill them, do we?" Kat asked.

"I don't see how we have a choice." Gol replied. "Unless you have a better idea."

Kat thought for a moment. "I have one idea." She crept out from behind the rocks where they were hiding for the moment and got as close as she could and sent out the weakest electric bolt she could, just enough to stun the dog. As the next dog came closer, she stunned that one too, and each one after that. Eventually they came at her in greater numbers and Gol had to come over and help her by stunning a few himself. Eventually the whole pack was unconscious. "We have to hurry they won't stay down for long."

They signaled back to their animals to stay put and wait for them to come back and they all crouched down behind the rocks out of sight. The two cyborgs crept into the city as cautiously as they could into the city. Once they started to get past the first buildings, they found the streets to be empty and silent. It was a surprise at first, but then they realized, the raid had required everyone in the Empire, not a single person was left in the city, only Emperor Zeke and his crew from his airship would be there.

Gol and Kat were relieved to think the empty streets would pose no threat of slowing them down. They soon found they were wrong, an alarm sounded, and robots were swarming them from every angle. Each one was just like the one that had helped Zeke escape, which meant that while they were dangerous, Gol and Kat already had experience fighting them. Once again, they had to use hand-held weapons, because their electric charges had been nearly exhausted, and they were sure they didn't have enough to fight all of them. It was going to be nothing but hack and slash the whole way, which meant the primary strategy was to run as fast as they could.

Gol and Kat soon realized that attempting to infiltrate the city without getting any information on the layout was a bad idea that they had carried out quite rashly. They didn't really know where they were going, their only clue was to go to the biggest and most centrally located building and hope they could find their way to Kyra from there. Navigating the streets was even harder with security drones hounding them every step of the way. Every time they outran or destroyed one, another one showed up.

Finally, they reached the central building, but their relief only lasted a moment. The front door was blocked by several robots. "Do you think we can take them?" Kat asked Gol.

Gol shook his head. "Not that many, not all at once, and not after we have been exhausted by our journey. We will have to find another way."

"Intruders!" Came the sound of a robot that had found them and was calling others to join.

"I guess we're doing this the hard way after all." Gol said as he drew his blades and attacked the first robot. Kat turned and fought the next one to approach them. They took turns cutting down as many robots as they could and trying to get to the door before they were killed.

Then there was another unfortunate surprise, as they neared the door, the last few robots got close together and initiated a transformation that resulted in becoming one larger robot. "I will give Zeke credit for this he knows how to put together enough dangerous machines to keep out those he doesn't want around."

"I think we can take this one though." Kat said.

"Really?" Gol asked. "How optimistic are you?"

"It's big but it's modular." Kat explained. "We just saw how it was put together it can come apart just as easily."

"Of course!" Gol replied. "They just combined, the points where they connect can't be that secure! If we aim for the joints, we can break them down!"

"Exactly!" Kat confirmed the strategy. "Let's do this!" They ran in to strike where the legs connected to the torso, knowing that was one of the weak points, and the first they could reach. As they approached, the mega robot threw blades at them. In the new configuration, the robots that were not the arms did not need their blades and those were being ejected as projectile weapons. Using the last of her electrical energy Kat deflected the blades that got too close to dodge. "That was all I've got, I have no juice left for anymore electrokinesis, it's going to be basic combat until I can recharge."

"No problem." Gol said. "We got this." Once they cut through the legs, the robot dropped to the ground but even though it lost its mobility, it was still attacking the cyborgs with its arms. They had to parry and counterattack each arm, but they were able to coordinate to keep the arms away from each other and fight them individually. With a synchronized attack at the shoulders, they were able to remove the arms and reduce the giant robot to a head and a helpless torso. At this point the robot started make a beeping sound while the eyes flashed. "That cannot be good, run inside quick!"

No sooner had Gol and Kat gotten inside the doors then the robot exploded. Even through the walls and closed doors, the shockwave knocked both cyborgs to the ground. Fortunately, the building was still sturdy enough to take the brunt of the blast. "Are you okay Kat?"

Kat dusted herself off and got up. "Yeah, a little shook up but fine. Let's go."

They approached the stairs but there were guards wielding gunblades waiting for them. It was the crew from the airship. Gol felt somewhat relieved that this was probably the last challenge between them and Zeke and Kyra, but at the same time, their exhaustion was setting in, Kat was out of power and Gol knew he didn't have much more left in him either. He looked Kat in the eye, she returned the look, and they nodded to each other. With weapons drawn they ran into battle ready to cut down every soldier that got in their way. The soldiers shot at them, but they moved in a zig zag behind columns, drawing the fire away so they wouldn't get hit and forcing the soldiers into close combat where they stood a better chance. Once they were close enough, they jumped into the fray, their determination bringing out something inside them, some sort of berserker rage that made them unstoppable and soon they cut down every single one until they were the only ones standing.

Now there was nothing left but to climb the stairs and meet the Emperor. The journey along the stairs felt slow and quiet compared to the journey to get here. But deep down, Gol and Kat knew this was only the calm before the storm, they were sure Zeke would be ready for them. He had been up until now and they had no doubt he was still ready for them. But they would not give up on their friend Kyra, not when they were so close. They approached the door of the throne room, knowing full well what they would find behind the door, but they could not stop now, they pushed the door open.

Inside they saw Kyra sitting on a throne, not the main throne, but a smaller, lesser throne. She wasn't just sitting on it, she was bound to the chair, her body wrapped in fabric woven into the chair, her cybernetic arm attached by cables that were clearly draining whatever energy the poor girl had left. She was wearing some sort of metal visor across her eyes secured to her head by two discs covering her ears. Next to her on the main throne sat Zeke. Even after his body was broken, he still had a look on his face like he was in charge and everyone was just a part of his show. His legs had been replaced and wires on the throne showed he was charging, but he smiled a wicked smile like he had never felt better or stronger than he did right now.

"Welcome!" Zeke laughed. "My old friends, welcome to my Empire! Please, allow me to get up and give you a proper greeting." Zeke pushed both of his hands against the arms of his chair and lifted himself up, tearing the wires apart behind him as he stepped forward. His body was now entirely encased in armor from the neck down, undoubtedly concealing the machinery required to operate his cybernetics. He was more machine than man, with a shiny chassis of chrome steel. He laughed maniacally. “Oh, how I have waited for this day, for this moment! Ever since the day of the exams, when my destiny was ripped from me and given to such undeserving peasants as you two!” Zeke pointed to Kyra with one hand and Gol with the other, but then dropped one hand and moved the other to point at Kat. “And then you of all people took pity on me and tried to help me when I was at my lowest. To insult me so, it was not enough to be humiliated by these two but even you had to act like you were better than me and in need of your mercy! I was born to be king, prince of the universe, the Technocracy was mine, my birthright all I had to do was claim it and you three reduced me to…nothing… exiled to dwell among gremlins on the fringes of society. But that was the best thing that ever happened to me, because once I was free of the Technocracy, I realized there was so much more that could be mine, I had been settling for our limited civilization, but now I could build my own with no limits! But the greatest reward of all is to share it with you all, to show you what I was capable of that you never were!”

“You’ve destroyed your land to build your Empire.” Gol said. “You grow no crops, you tend no livestock, your water is undrinkable, your air is unbreathable. You have proven the Technocracy was right by ignoring their caution. What kind of accomplishment is that?”

Zeke continued laughing, in his madness it did not seem that he could stop for any length of time. “That’s why I came back to invade the Technocracy, to take all of that from them.”

“And then what?” Gol asked. “What happens when you destroy our land too?”

Zeke shrugged. “Then I move on the next piece of land.”

“And what happens when you run out of land?” Gol asked. “What happens when you have turned the whole world into a barren wasteland?”

"It will never come to that." Zeke said, beginning to sour.

"At this rate you will!" Gol shouted, brandishing his blades. "Unless someone stops you!"

Now Zeke had lost any pretense of pleasantness. "You just don't understand progress! Do you know what we have accomplished here, what we have built? All the technology the Technocracy has forbidden has been made reality! Nothing is impossible!"

"Nothing comes without a price!" Gol said. "And the price you have paid for your Empire is too heavy! Your people are too blind to see it, that's why you were all exiled."

"Enough!" Zeke screamed while releasing his cyberblades. "I have tolerated you thus far because I was looking forward to your astonishment at how my success has eclipsed yours and you've just taken all the fun out of it! Let's end this!" He then launched into an attack on Gol and Kat.

Although Zeke had been rebuilt with more raw power and Gol and Kat were tired, his anger blinded him to reason, and he had lost his edge. He was a savage beast, but Gol and Kat were prepared to fight back. At first, they toyed with him a little to try to wear him out and even things out. The two moved in perfect sync as if they were one and nothing Zeke could do seemed to pierce their defenses. Once they had his pattern of movements down and he started slowing a bit, Kat slipped away to help Kyra and Gol took over the duel. Zeke tried to pursue Kat for a moment, but Gol intercepted him. "No you don't! Your fight is with me!"

Zeke merely growled in response his rage had rendered him mute at this point. While the duel was going on between the two men, Kat went to free Kyra. First, she removed the visor because that was the easiest part, then disconnected the wires holding her cyberarm because that was still easier than trying to figure out how to free her from the fabric wrapped around her body. This part was trickier than it looked because it was so tight that a wrong cut could hurt her more than help her. Once the bindings were cut free of the chair, Kat tried to lift Kyra off and carry her. Kyra had been so drained that she couldn't move on her own. The fabric started to fall from her body, and she was wearing little underneath. "He stripped you too? What the hell is wrong with this guy?" Kat mustered her strength, draped her friend over her shoulders and dragged her across the hall, trying to get her to the door without Zeke stopping her. Gol managed to keep Zeke distracted until Kat and Kyra almost reached the door.

Kat was just a few steps away from the door when Zeke caught her out of the corner of his eye. He turned his attention to the women to try to stop them from escaping, but in that moment of distraction, Gol took advantage of his weakness and struck him with all his electrical energy concentrated into his cyberblade. The blow hit a hole in Zeke's armor where his charger cable had been plugged in at the cross section of his internal power cables that powered his right arm and his legs. It was supposed to merely incapacitate Zeke, but Gol had moved too fast and stuck too hard. When he checked Zeke's pulse, he was dead.

Kat set Kyra down and came over to Gol. "It was him or us. He did it to himself. Now, Kyra needs us, let's go." Together they carried Kyra out of the building and through the city back to their silverwings. The other animals were waiting safely, the guard dogs were unconscious and covered in slime, the slime itself had a deceptively innocent look in its eyes that wasn't fooling anybody. They didn't have time to be anything but grateful that their ride home was safe, so they put Kyra on Kat's bird and began their long journey back home.

As the cyborgs fled, lights flickered in the empty throne room behind them and a robot that had been lying dormant and unnoticed in the back blinked to life.

Chapter 15

Retracing their steps, they found they were much safer on the return trip since they knew what to avoid. As they came within sight of home, the war was still raging on. Fortunately for the travelers, the soldiers being actively engaged in the battle meant that they were not in the camp to prevent Gol, Kat, and Kyra from getting through. They took advantage of the moment to cross the battle lines and get back to their side. However, returning home also meant entering the city while it was under siege. The soldiers were everywhere, and no place was safe.

"What do we do now?" Gol said. "We definitely don't have the energy to fight one more battle."

Kat paused in thought, feeling as distraught as Gol did. Then she brightened up when an idea hit her. "We can't fight anymore, but I know who might still have the energy! Let's go to the Menagerie!"

"We can go through the sewers." Gol said. "We can enter through the outlet by the river and go straight to the Menagerie underground. All the cleanup they need to do, they must have a major drain right there we can exit through."

"Perfect!" Kat agreed. "Or at least as close as we can get right now!" Kat turned her bird to the river and Gol followed along. The sewer was the safest route, the imperial troops hadn't considered going down there so it was all clear until they got to the Menagerie.

Once they emerged, Gol was curious about Kat's plan. "What do we do now?"

Kat laughed. "I would have thought you would have figured that out by now. There's only one thing here that we can put to our advantage." She started walking toward the particular habitat she had in mind, and her plan became obvious.

Gol suddenly figured out Kat's plan. "No, you aren't serious right now?"

"Unless you have a better idea." Kat replied as she opened the cage where their dragons were staying with the phoenix. She brought Kyra to the phoenix. "The phoenix has restorative qualities, and it can fight to protect itself and Kyra. This will be the safest place we can leave her. Kewpie, carbuncle, the slime and our birds can stay here with them. Syldra will keep watch over all of them so nobody will hurt her, right girl?" The dragon gave a proud screech and spread her wings in a defensive gesture of Kyra and the animals huddled around her.

"And where do you think we are going?" Gol asked even though he knew the answer before he even began to speak.

"We're going to ride our dragons into battle and settle this!" Kat said. "Go and get Bahamut. Come on Leviathan! Ready to spread your wings and enjoy some open air?"

The dragons had grown rather quickly since they hatched, in just a few years they were now twice the size of a silverwing and more than capable of carrying a fully grown cyborg, and Bahamut was the largest of the three. So far, they hadn't actually tried flying, at most they had cuddled with their dragons when they were little and rested on their backs when they got larger. It was going to be trial by fire, literally.

Gol was somewhat wary, but the dragons were eager to spread their wings and fly. At first the two dragons managed to take to the sky without notice but as they were steered toward the action, the dragons breathed fire at any large gatherings of soldiers. When the soldiers were spread out and mixed with the Technocratic allies, the dragons held their fire and picked them off with their fangs and talons instead. When the Imperial airships joined the fray, the dragons started attacking them too. The airships proved useless without their propellers and balloons.

There were only two dragons, but that's all it took to rally the troops and turn the tide. Every Hunter and fencer redoubled their efforts and pushed back the imperial troops. Some of the imperials tried to hold their ground and it became clear that they did not know their Emperor was dead. Once this thought occurred to Gol and Kat, they started shouting it out hoping the soldiers could hear them. "Your Emperor is dead, and so is your Empire! The war is over!"

It took time to push back all the soldiers, not all of them could hear what Gol and Kat were saying or have the good sense to retreat from the dragons. But as the soldiers became isolated from each other, they slowly realized that they had lost and retreated.

But then, just when it seemed like the war was ending, a shadow appeared in the sky. At first it appeared to be growing larger, but it was actually coming closer. The closer it came, the clearer it was that it was another dragon. It came directly for Gol and as it approached, it had a rider, a figure painfully familiar to Gol. It was all metal, no skin visible, no flesh left to show, it was a robot through and through to be sure, but his presence was unmistakable even in this new body. "Zeke?"

"Zeke is no more!" The rider replied. "Call me Omega, for I am the end of all! Destroy them all Tiamat! Destroy them all!" Omega, formerly Zeke, said no more, silently directing his mount to kill everyone, starting with the other dragons and their riders.

"Why won't you just die?" Gol called. "I once considered you a friend and mourned your loss, but you have gone too far! Stop!"

"I am beyond death!" Omega replied, his voice booming across the sky over the Technocratic capital. "I have traded mortal flesh for eternal metal and circuits! I am immortal, I am a god!" Omega went silent again, trying to goad the imperial troops on for another onslaught. Some followed their Emperor, but many did not move from their camp. They were exhausted and seeing the machine riding a dragon did not encourage them, but rather frightened them. They did not see their Emperor with hope, they saw a dead man living, a horrible abomination that was bringing nothing but destruction. The imperial soldiers had surrendered.

A second legion came, this one consisting of robots. Some came on foot, others came by airship and dropped in from the sky. Where those with weak human hearts failed, the cold unfeeling machines carried on. But the Technocratic Militia were resilient, they would not give up protecting their homes and loved ones. No matter how weary they were they would not surrender the city to these invaders.

Gol and Kat directed their dragons focus on taking down the new wave of airships and managed to stop about half the troops in midair. Once the airships were taken out, it was down to just the three dragons to fight in the sky. While the Hunters and Fencers fought the robots on the ground, Gol and Kat fought their leader in the sky to settle their fates once and for all. Omega was ruthless, and Gol and Kat had to be as well. Tiamat kept breathing fire at them and the other dragons kept veering off away and trying to shoot back around the attacks that were coming for them. The counter-attack strategy was working quite well, the blind rage that the enemy was attacking with meant that each attack was leaving Tiamat and Omega wide open and vulnerable, and Gol and Kat took advantage of every opportunity to have Bahamut and Leviathan strike back. Eventually, all three dragons grew weary, Tiamat gave up first and crashed into the fencing arena. Gol and Kat brought Bahamut and Leviathan down to rest on the ground so they could check on Omega, they wanted to make sure he wasn't getting back up again.

Unfortunately, Omega did rise from behind Tiamat's motionless body, his cyberblades drawn. "Let's end this!" He came straight for Gol.

Gol drew his blades and parried Omega's attack. It took everything to block the strike, there was a very heavy force behind it. "Is it just that you are too angry to die?" Gol asked Zeke. "How is it possible that you are still alive? I killed you, I checked your pulse, I watched you die."

"You killed my flesh yes." Omega replied. "But I had backed up my mind. Our cybernetics rely on circuitry that mimics our natural nervous system. If you have enough circuits to make a large enough machine, you can copy a brain. It took some time to condense that data into a normal size body, but fortunately I had this back-up plan in the works for a while and this was ready for my untimely death. And if you destroy my body I will be back again, I just need time to make another, but my mind will last forever! I will last forever!" With an overabundance of confidence, Omega continued to attack Gol.

The three cyborgs were once again locked into a continuous cyclical fight, with Gol and Omega dueling and Kat trying to keep Gol safe and alive until the fight ended. Omega was stronger now than when he was merely Zeke, he didn't tire at the same pace as his opponents, he kept going at an unstoppable pace.

"Gol, we can't keep going on like this." Kat said. "But I can help you finish it." Kat channeled all her electrical energy into Gol, a feat which exhausted her, and she passed out.

Gol perked up, filled with enough energy to fight Omega for a few more rounds as strong as when they started. Gol even had enough energy in him to keep Omega occupied enough to get him away from Kat. However, it did not last, soon Gol was faltering again.

"Are you ready to give up?" Omega asked as he was about to strike the final blow on his exhausted opponent.

"No!" Angus called. "We will never give up!" He was too far away to fight Omega himself, so he channeled his electrical energy to help Gol fight. Biggs, Wedge, and Mack followed suit right behind Angus. Soon everybody was channeling their power to Gol. A great thunderstorm formed over the battlefield, with Gol in the eye of the storm. Gol channeled all this electricity into his blade and focused it on Omega. Omega was blasted several body lengths away by the force of the blast, debris collapsing on him upon impact. The pulse was enough to deactivate all the robots fighting under Omega. With all the imperial cyborgs having surrendered, the war was officially over.

Gol and his companions barely managed to smile, satisfied that Omega had finally been defeated. Then, after a few minutes, there was motion. Omega stood again, beaten, battered, and with wires sticking out of holes in his armor, but still functioning.

"In the name of Hinu!" Gol exclaimed. "Why won't you just die?"

Omega approached Gol. There was nothing more that could be done, everyone had used all their energy. The imperials that had surrendered had given their all as well. Omega stumbled towards Gol about to finally strike the final blow when another dragon arrived. Kyra was riding Syldra landing between Gol and Omega. Omega looked Syldra in the face, and as the dragon's mouth opened, it was the last thing Omega saw.

Chapter 16

Zeke woke up in a familiar four-poster bed in an equally familiar room. He wasn't sure how he got here, he couldn't remember anything. The only thought he had was Kyra, but he couldn't even remember why that mattered. Then she appeared, coming around the corner of his field of vision. "You're awake. Good, I thought you would never wake up."

"How did we get here?" Zeke asked. "I could have sworn this isn't where we left off."

Kyra laughed. "Of course it is silly. Where else would we be? This is our home."

Zeke shook his head. "No, we had an argument, you didn't want this."

"I changed my mind." Kyra replied. "I realized you were right. This is paradise. I want to spend my life here with you my dear." She took his face in her hands and kissed him. "Please, just you and me, here in our palace of dreams forever."

Zeke smiled and felt satisfied. But the satisfaction did not last. He knew this did not make sense this could not be real. Kyra could not have changed her mind so suddenly. "No this is not real. You didn't want to be here. I hoped you would come around but...no, not like this, not this quickly. It's just not possible. I missed something. What did I miss? Why did you change your mind?"

Kyra finally broke her smile. "Okay, I wanted this to go easy, but if you insist on the truth, I came back with you for the sake of peace. The war was hurting the Technocracy and the Empire and I didn't want anyone else to get hurt, so I'm here because I hope that if you have me here, it will be enough and you will stop your siege."

"Of course you would try to stop me and negotiate peace." Zeke said. "But don't think it will be that simple. I will not simply live a lie!"

"Why not?" Kyra replied. "You expected me to do it. You promised this was all that we needed."

"Enough!" Zeke said. "I will claim the real world, and then I will come back once my Empire has been established! You can wait for me here." Zeke activated his option to log out and return to the real world. In the blink of an eye, the simulacrum faded out and Zeke was in his throne room. Looking to his side, Kyra was there, wearing her headset. Zeke unplugged himself, then unplugged Kyra.

Kyra's visor came loose and fell away. Her face was distressed, she had clearly been crying. "Okay, we're back in the real world, is this enough for you?"

"I said I would take the Technocracy, and I will not settle until I do!" Zeke said getting up and leaving the throne room. He went to go get Tiamat, but she was not in her nest. "Where is Tiamat?"

"She was wounded, and we had to leave her back in Technocracy territory." Kyra explained. "The Beastmasters are caring for her at the Menagerie. I can go back for her when she is fully recovered."

"She is my dragon!" Zeke exclaimed. "I will not leave her to another! I will go back by airship and collect her! And where is everyone else?"

Kyra shook her head. "Nobody else made it back from the war. They all either died or defected."

Zeke was infuriated. "Fine! Then I will make do with robots!" He went to his control room and recalled a crew of robots from the city patrol and boarded his airship to fly back to the Technocracy. As he made the flight, something went wrong. The world around him became distorted and broke apart in hexagonal pieces with a green glowing halo.

Zeke found himself in his throne room again, just as before. He looked to his side and Kyra was there again removing her visor. "Is something wrong Zeke?"

"It was another simulation?!" Zeke exclaimed.

"I'm sorry but I wasn't sure I could trust you not to go back to war." Kyra pleaded. "Please, I promise to stay if you promise to let go of this war."

"Is Tiamat really in the Menagerie?" Zeke asked.

Kyra shook her head. "No, she's in her nest downstairs."

Zeke rushed to find Tiamat in her nest. Climbing on her back he prodded her to fly away back to the Technocracy. As they arrived back at the Technocratic capital, they found nobody was on the ground. Zeke looked everywhere for anyone. He was sure there was more to do here, but there was nobody, no enemies, no allies, nothing. "No, not again."

Kyra approached him. "You're right, it is annoying when someone keeps going past the boundaries of your simulation before you're ready for them. And programming anything alive, especially people, is very hard."

"How many layers are there to this simulation?" Zeke asked.

"As many as you need." Kyra replied.

"Need?" Zeke asked. "What would I need all of these layers for?"

"Until you give up." Kyra answered.

Zeke realized what she meant and panicked. "Access user menu."

"That won't work." Kyra replied. "I disabled that option for you, the computer no longer recognizes you as the user, so you can't access the code anymore."

Zeke got up and ran. He went to an underground corridor and kept running to the end until he found a door and opened it. The room he was expecting was not there, instead it was just empty space. When he turned back, he saw Kyra again. "The back door? I removed that too. Can't have you just editing this from the inside without me."

Zeke got desperate and tried to disconnect himself manually and force himself to log out. Again, the world shattered, and he found himself in his throne room again.

Kyra was next to him, removing her visor. "Is something wrong Zeke?"

"Am I still in the simulation?" Zeke asked.

Kyra's face broke into a wide grin. "Yes."

Zeke once again tried to force a logout, and once again, the scene reset in the throne room.

Kyra was next to him, removing her visor. "Is something wrong Zeke?"

"Am I still in the simulation?" Zeke asked.

Kyra's face broke into a wide grin. "Yes."

Zeke once again tried to force a logout, and once again, the scene reset in the throne room.

Kyra was next to him, removing her visor. "Is something wrong Zeke?"

"Am I still in the simulation?" Zeke asked.

Kyra's face broke into a wide grin. "Yes."

Zeke once again tried to force a logout, and once again, the scene reset in the throne room.

Kyra was next to him, removing her visor. "Is something wrong Zeke?"

"Am I still in the simulation?" Zeke asked.

Kyra's face broke into a wide grin. "Yes."

Zeke once again tried to force a logout, and once again, the scene reset in the throne room.

Kyra was next to him, removing her visor. "Is something wrong Zeke?"

"Am I still in the simulation?" Zeke asked.

Kyra's face broke into a wide grin. "Yes."

Zeke once again tried to force a logout.

Kyra interrupted him. "We can do this all day." She was still grinning.

"Let me out!" Zeke screamed. "I want to go back to my body!"

"What body?" Kyra asked.

"Huh?" Zeke asked. "What do you mean? I mean I want to be put back into my body in the real world!"

"That is not possible." Kyra replied.

"Why not?" Zeke asked.

"You don't have a body anymore." Kyra answered. "You died in this throne room. You chose to load the last of what was left of your mind into an artificial body, and you used that for one last attack. We destroyed that body. And after all that madness, why do you think we would ever give you access to any physical body ever again?"

"Then why did you load me back here?" Zeke asked.

"Because you were so relentless, we figured it would be best if we could put you somewhere we knew you wouldn't be a threat anymore."

"And why are you here?" Zeke asked.

Kyra did not respond at first. She looked away, then looked back with a somehow wider grin. "Programming people into the simulation is hard...but not impossible."

The truth finally dawned on Zeke. "You're not really here, are you?" Zeke asked.

Kyra paused again. "Do you really need me to answer that one?"

Zeke tried to cry, but the simulation wouldn't allow it. "Why?"

"Well, if you had accepted the first version, or the second, or even the third, maybe you could have just lived in bliss believing this world was real. Or you could have stopped sooner before it even got as far as you getting stuck in a simulation in the first place. But nothing was ever enough for you. Your father knew this and that's why he cut you off in the first place. You did this to yourself, and you could have stopped anytime, all you had to do was accept your own limitations. But instead, here we are. Just you and me in your little paradise, just the way you wanted it."

"Except it isn't you and me." Zeke said. "It's just me. You're not really here."

"Well, I guess I could take Tiamat and leave you really alone." Kyra said. "Or do you want us to keep you company here?"

"No, no, please stay!" Zeke said, suddenly afraid of the loneliness and isolation. "Don't leave me alone!"

"Okay, I'll stay." Kyra said with her smile returning. "But you must play nice, or I'll take my dragon and go home. Just one last question: Do you want to stay here or go back to the other version of the palace?"

Zeke looked around at the more realistic version of the palace, how dark and depressing it was. He could ignore it when he believed there were other places he could go, but now that he knew he would never leave, he realized this wasn't where he wanted to spend the rest of his life after all. That's why he had built this simulation and made the original version so much better than what he could cobble together in reality. "Can we take Tiamat to the other one?"

Kyra snapped her fingers to make the transition. "As you wish!"

Chapter 17

Kyra pushed herself away from the control panel. "That should keep him out of our hair for the foreseeable future. Now we just need to go back and get to work rebuilding the Technocracy."

"And take care of the orphans." Kat added. "While you were working on the simulation, Gol and I went looking around the city. We found that a few families got started here in the Empire, all the children were hiding in shelters while their parents were out at war. We're going to try to reunite as many as we can with their parents, assuming they survived, but the rest are going to have a hard time."

"I'm sure we can figure out something for them." Kyra replied optimistically. "We can start an orphanage and we'll see how many kids get adopted. I'm just glad none of them were hurt during the war."

"Are we ready to go home now?" Gol asked the Kyra and Kat.

Kyra let out a heavy sigh. "Yes. I think we took care of everything we need to take care of here."

The three friends left the control room of the simulation facility. Despite Zeke's fixation on the palace and the city, this facility was built on a mountain peak on the far side of the Empire, far from anyone that might ever disturb it. He had intended for this to be a security measure to keep anyone from bothering him, but now it would be his prison to make sure nobody ever freed him. His remains, both flesh and cybernetic were kept here now, most importantly his brain, or rather the cybernetic facsimile of his brain. His mind had been hardwired into this computer to spend the rest of his life inside the artificial world he had created. His body, including his severed limbs, were being kept in a glass tank filled with liquid nitrogen. Thanks to the cold temperatures at the high altitude, his flesh would remain undisturbed indefinitely. As Zeke said, there were solar panels on the roof that would make sure this facility could operate indefinitely, so as the door was closed, Zeke would be left to his own devices forever.

Gol, Kat, and Kyra had made the journey on their dragons and flew back down to the city to find the children and the dogs that were all that was left living in the Empire. Decidedly innocent victims, none older than seven years of age, they were all going to the Technocracy for a fresh start. They gathered and walked the trail between the two countries, following the dragons flying overhead. The caravan carefully navigated around the various hazards on the road. When they crossed the boundary between the two lands, the children were all amazed.

"What is that bright thing in the sky?"

"Why is the sky blue?"

"Where did the clouds go?"

"Why is everything so green?"

"What are these big birds everywhere?"

"Even the water looks different! It smells different too!"

It was painfully clear their home had been damaged for as long as any of them could remember and a healthy landscape was unfamiliar to them. Those whose parents were still alive were reunited with their families who were waiting for them at the border. The rest were redirected to the Temple of the Healers where they would be treated for malnourishment and exposure to toxins. The older children would eventually be enrolled at the Academy as boarding students to become productive members of society. The parents still had a debt to pay off to society, but enough blood had been shed and the survivors were not going to suffer for their crimes, at least not as long as they were willing to work on post war repairs. Those who were not willing to work had their cybernetics removed and were forced to work anyway and when they weren't working, they were sent to the dungeon under the city. Most joined the Hunter's Guild because they had knowledge of the wilderness and made great guides.

Once everything settled down, an important meeting was called at the High Council. Most of the meeting was the expected discussion regarding the refugees and reparations, but Chancellor Cidolfas surprised everyone with an announcement. "I am going to step down as Chancellor, I am retiring. However, I will not leave you all without leadership. Kyra, please come up here."

Kyra was shocked, this felt very unexpected. As she approached, she could hardly believe what was happening. "Me? You're choosing me to be the next Chancellor?"

Cidolfas nodded. "Don't be so surprised dear, I told you as much your first day."

Kyra blushed and lowered her head. "That seems like just yesterday."

Cidolfas raised her head. "Chin up my dear. Honestly my girl, I have had a good feeling about you since your exams. I hand-picked you to be my apprentice and all these years you have worked under me since I have been testing you as much as training you to take my place. You have proven beyond any of my doubts that you are worthy of leading our people. Now the only question is do you feel ready?"

Kyra looked around the room at all the important people gathered, all the people who would look to her for guidance, the Engineers, the Smiths, and the Guildmasters. And then her eyes fell on the only people she knew she could truly count on, Gol and Kat, who she had brought along for moral support. They both nodded at her, and she smiled. "Yes, I am ready sir!"

Cidolfas removed the ceremonial circlet from his head and placed it upon hers, and gave her his medallion as well, to complete the ceremony. "I hereby appoint you, Kyra, Chancellor of the Technocracy!"

The whole council gave Kyra a standing ovation and it brought her to tears.

As they left the council meeting, Kat took Gol's hand in hers. "Now where were we before all of this? I believe you were going to marry me."

Gol nodded. "Yes, I do believe that is where we left off."

"Well?" Kat prodded.

"Well, what?" Gol asked

"Well, when are we going to get married?" Kat prodded further. "Or did you change your mind?"

Gol laughed and shook his head. "No, I didn't change my mind at all. Let's get on those wedding plans as soon as possible."

"Can those plans include the new Chancellor officiating the ceremony?" Kyra interrupted from behind them.

They turned to face her. Kat spoke first. "We would be honored!"

* * *

Time flew by for Gol and the next thing he knew he was being prepared for his wedding. Angus was his best man with help from Biggs and Wedge. He was dressed in his gator skin armor, buffed and polished to a shine. With a white cloak to complete his noble look. He was marched down the aisle at the Temple to wait by the altar with Kyra. He looked out at the guests, all the friends he and Kat had made over the years around the city. It wasn't until this moment that he realized how many lives they had touched and how many of them touched his life. But they all seemed to disappear when his bride came down the aisle to meet him.

She was an absolute vision in her white gown and veil, both with pink trim hinting at her vocation as a Healer. Her hair had been styled perfectly to frame her face, her lipstick the perfect shade to accentuate her lips around her smile, her eyelashes accentuated by mascara to draw attention to the eyes that were focused on him as much as he was focused on her.

Gol spoke his vows first. "Kat, my love, as a Smith I have built a great many things, but nothing greater than the life I will build with you."

Then it was Kat's turn. "Gol, my love, I have pursued many adventures as a Healer, but the greatest adventure is yet to come, and I look forward to every step of it by your side."

They sealed their vows with a kiss, and everyone cheered. The reception was one of the best feasts the Technocracy had ever seen, everyone celebrating the heroes of the war. The feast was held at the Menagerie like Kat had wanted. There was a nice garden area Gol didn't know about until they setup their wedding there, but it was perfect, with just the right flowers in full bloom and birds flying overhead that Kat refused to either confirm or deny if she had them arranged. Music was played by the finest bards and minstrels in the Technocracy. They ate, drank and danced the night away. As the party started to wind down, their parents came to check on them. "What are you planning to do next?" Gol's father asked.

"Can we be expecting grandkids anytime soon?" Gol's mother added.

"I've been waiting to be a grandma!" Kat's mother added.

"Calm down ladies, you'll scare them!" Kat's father interjected.

Ruby joined in. "Are we going to have another little Healer on our hands?"

"Or a little Smith?" Angus added.

Kat shook her head. "No, none of that! We're going to see the world!"

"Yeah, getting out of the Technocracy during the war opened our eyes." Gol said. "There is so much out there we have never seen, that maybe nobody has ever seen. Zeke's Empire was just the edge of the world we know, we want to see what goes beyond that."

"So tomorrow we pack up our silverwings and hit the open road!" Kat said.

Ruby smiled. "Well Hinu bless you on your journey!"

"Safe travels!" Angus added. "And don't worry, I'll make sure the rebuilding continues smoothly in your absence." Angus added half-jokingly, as if Gol and Kat were that critical that the realm would cease functioning without them.

With tears in their eyes, they hugged their mentors. "Thank you so much!" Kat said to Ruby.

"For everything." Gol said to Angus.

* * *

As the sun rose the next day, Gol and Kat prepared for their next adventure just as they said. Gol had Kewpie on his silverwing, Kat had her carbuncle on her silverwing and all the supplies they needed for the road ahead, at least for a few days until they could find some new food. Everyone came to see them off by the city gate. Everyone was tearing up as they said their goodbyes. They could hardly get the words out. The last was Kyra. "Good luck my friends, may we meet again."

"It's not goodbye forever." Kat said, reassuring her friend. "We will come around again. And I am sure you will be the best Chancellor the technocracy has ever had."

Trumpets blared as the city gave a send-off to their two heroes. And watched them disappear over the horizon.

* * *

Cidolfas rode Tiamat to his son's tomb to say one last farewell. He looked at the body floating frozen in its cryonic chamber. He sat down by the control panel and put the visor on to enter the simulation. "Zeke?"

"Father?" Zeke replied when he saw him. "Is it really you?"

"Yes, my son." Cidolfas replied.

He appeared like he was going to cry. "You're not just another simulacrum like Kyra and Tiamat?"

Cidolfas shook his head and laughed a little. "No, it's really me son."

"What brings you here?" Zeke asked.

"I just wanted to ask you one question." Cidolfas replied.

"Sure, anything father." Zeke replied. "Ask away."

Cidolfas smiled. "How did you get the airships to work?"

www.ingramcontent.com/pod-product-compliance
Lightning Source LLC
LaVergne TN
LVHW010553160826
845677LV00013B/3118

* 9 7 9 8 3 7 2 9 8 9 2 9 0 *